14

JUNIOR

CLASSICS

Published by
Rupa Publications India Pvt. Ltd 2016
7/16, Ansari Road, Daryaganj
New Delhi 110002

Sales centres:
Bengaluru Chennai
Hyderabad Jaipur Kathmandu
Kolkata Mumbai Prayagraj

ISBN: 978-81-291-3898-9

Third impression 2023

10 9 8 7 6 5 4 3

Printed in India

Contents

Golden Dreams

Washington Irving

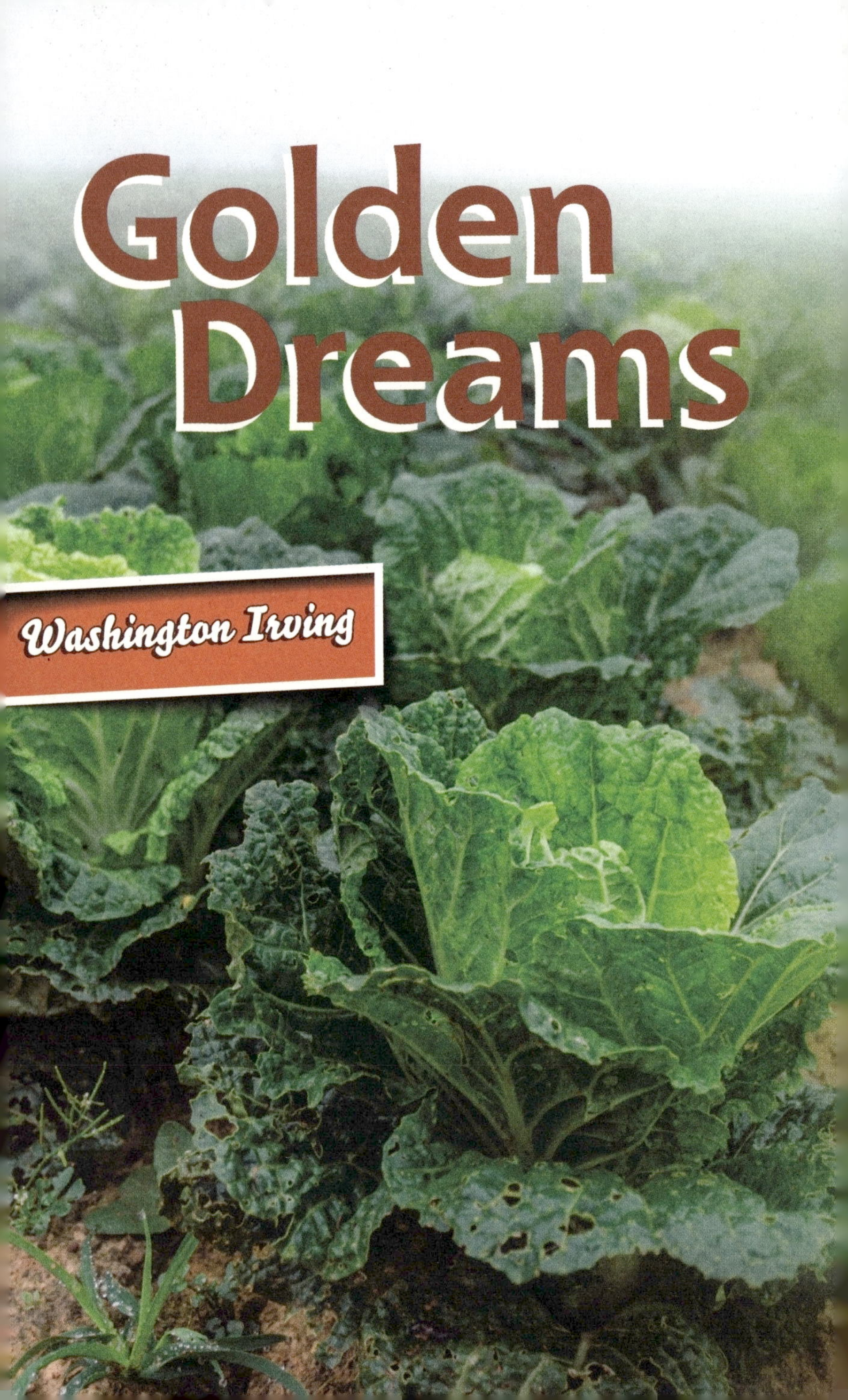

Somewhere in the early part of the eighteenth century, there lived in the city of Manhattoes a man called Wolfert Webber. He was a descendant of the Dutchman Cobus Webber, one of the original settlers, who was famous for introducing the cultivation of cabbages to America. The Webber family still owned the field in which Cobus Webber planted his first cabbages. The family continued to grow cabbages, and several generations devoted their lives to the study and development of this one noble vegetable. As a result, the cabbages from the Webber family farm were gigantic, and became very famous.

Even as the generations passed, the family continued to live in its ancestral mansion: a Dutch-built house, with a front-end of yellow brick, tapering to a point, with the customary iron weathercock at the top. Everything about the building bore the air of long-settled ease and security. Birds packed the little coops nailed against the walls, and built their nests under the eaves—a sure sign of good luck to the family that hosts them. On bright sunny days, the air was filled with their cheerful notes, as they played and chirped in the pure sweet air. Thus, the excellent family prospered under the shade of a mighty buttonwood tree, which by little and little grew so great as entirely to overshadow their palace. The city gradually spread around their home. First, houses sprung, then villages, and eventually, a whole city. Still, however, the Webbers maintained their character and possessions. Wolfert was the last of the line, a kind of rural ruler in the midst of a city.

His wife was one of those excellent 'stirring women'—one of those notable little housewives who are always busy when there is nothing to do. Her whole life was devoted to intense knitting; whether at home or abroad; walking or sitting, her needles were continually in motion, and her knitting kept the whole household supplied with stockings throughout the year. This worthy couple were blessed with one daughter, who was brought up with great tenderness and care. She could stitch, make all kinds of pickles and preserves, and even write her own name. Her influence was also seen in the family garden, where whole rows of fiery marigolds and splendid hollyhocks bordered the cabbage-beds; and

gigantic sunflowers hung their broad, jolly faces loosely over the fences, seeming to watch most affectionately the passers-by.

Thus Wolfert Webber reigned over his land, peaceably and contentedly. However, he did have his own share of problems, like any ruler. As his territory gradually became surrounded by streets and houses, his lands were occasionally raided; sometimes by children, and sometimes by pigs. These vagrants would carry off his best cabbages, and behead the sunflowers. Still all these were minor problems to which Wolfert Webber had a simple solution. He kept a trusty staff just behind the front door; and, at the first sight of trouble, would grab it, rush out and hit the trespasser—both children and pigs—on the back, and return inside.

Wolfert's biggest worry was that, as the city prospered, living expenses went up drastically. However, he could not grow any more cabbages, nor could he increase his prices. Thus, as everyone around him grew richer, Wolfert grew poorer, and he could not, for the life of him, figure out how to solve this problem. This growing worry eventually caused wrinkles on his forehead—something unheard of among his ancestors.

Perhaps even this would not have disturbed him so much if he had only himself and his wife to care for. However, there was his daughter Amy gradually growing to maturity; and everyone knows that daughters require so much looking after as they grow up. I have no talent at describing female charms, and so will not depict the progress of this little Dutch beauty: how her blue eyes grew deeper and deeper, and her cherry lips redder and redder. By the time she was seventeen, she resembled a half-blown rose-bud, dressed in traditional Dutch finery, with her hair smoothened with buttermilk and a chain of yellow virgin gold encircling her neck.

Anyway, she had reached that age where she was drawing hearts in her notebooks and embroidering lover's knots in deep blue silk and generally looking for more interesting things to do than grow sunflowers and make pickles.

At this critical period, when the female heart is easily engrossed, a new visitor began to frequent the Webber home. This was Dirk Waldron, the good-looking son of a poor widow; she had been married four times, but Dirk was her only son.

This youngster gradually became a frequent visitor at the Webber household. He talked little, but he sat for long periods. He filled the father's pipe when it was empty, gathered up the mother's knitting needle, or ball of wool when it fell to the ground; stroked the sleek coat of the tortoise-shell cat, and replenished the teapot for the daughter from the bright copper kettle that sung before the fire. These little errands may not seem important, but when true love is translated into Low Dutch, this is how it appears. Dirk's efforts were not wasted. The youngster found marvellous favour in the eyes of the mother; the tortoise-shell cat approved of him, and the tea-kettle seemed to sing out a cheering note of welcome, and the sly glances of the daughter showed that she liked him as well.

Wolfert alone saw nothing of what was going on. Wrapped up as he was in thoughts about the growing city and his cabbages, he sat looking into the fire, and puffing his pipe in silence.

One night, however, even Wolfert's dull ears were startled by the noise of the goodnight kiss between Amy and Dirk. Thus, the father had a new source of worry. It had never entered into his head that this 'child'—who he remembered climbing onto his knees and playing with dolls not too long ago—could all at once be thinking of love and marriage.

He rubbed his eyes, thought about it and

decided that, while he had been dreaming of other matters, his little Amy had actually grown into a woman, and fallen in love.

Wolfert was a kind father, but he was also a reasonable man. He liked the young man, but the young man had neither money nor land. Wolfert considered the options and found that, if the young couple married, he would have to give them a portion of his cabbage garden, the whole of which was barely enough to support the family!

Like a responsible father, therefore, he decided to nip their passion in the bud. So he banned Dirk from the house, even though he did not like to do so. Amy cried silently, but followed her father's wishes. She did not pout or sulk; she never rebelled, or fell into hysterics. Instead, she complied like an obedient daughter; shut the street-door on her lover's face; and if ever she did speak to him, it was either out of the kitchen window, or over the garden fence.

Wolfert was deeply pondering these things in his mind, and his brow wrinkled with unusual care, as he made his way one Saturday afternoon to a rural inn, about two miles from the city. It was a favourite among the Dutch community since it had always been run by Dutch landlords and retained an air of the 'good old times'.

It was a Dutch-built house, which had probably been the home of some opulent denizen in the early days. The venerable and somewhat crazy mansion was distinguished from afar, by a grove of elms and sycamores that seemed to wave hospitably to welcome visitors. A few weeping willows with their dank, drooping foliage, resembling falling waters, gave an idea of coolness, and rendered it an attractive spot during the heat of summer.

This inn, as I said, was often frequented by the Dutch inhabitants of the city, some of whom came here to play shuffle-board and quoits and ninepins, while others came to smoke a deliberate pipe, and talk about public affairs.

It was on a windy autumn afternoon that Wolfert made his visit to the inn. The grove of

elms and willows was naked without its leaves, which whirled about the fields.

The bowling alley was deserted, for the unseasonal cold had driven the inn's patrons to seek the warmth of the fireplace indoors. As it was Saturday afternoon, the place was full of its Dutch regulars although there were some others of various character and country. Beside the fireplace, Ramm Rapelye sat in a huge leather armchair, lording over his little domain. He was a Walloon, well known for his long ancestral line; his great grandmother had been the first white child born in the province. He was even better known for his wealth and dignity: he had long been active in local politics, and was a man to whom the governor himself took off his hat. He had occupied the huge leather chair for years; and had gradually grown in bulk until he filled it. He ruled the inn from this chair, and his word was decisive with his subjects; for he was so rich a man, that he was never expected to support any opinion by argument. The landlord waited on him with particular care; not that he paid better than his neighbours, but then the coin of a rich man seems always to be so much more acceptable. The landlord had always a pleasant word and a joke, to whisper in his ear. The august Ramm never laughed, and generally maintained a mastiff-like gravity. Yet, now and then, he rewarded the host with a kind of grunt, which delighted the landlord more than a broad laugh from a poorer man.

When Wolfert entered, he heard the landlord say, 'This will be a rough night for the money-diggers.'

A gust of wind howled round the house, and rattled at the windows.

'What, are they at it again?' said a one-eyed English captain, who was a regular at the inn.

'Aye, they are,' said the landlord, 'and well may they be. They've had luck lately. They say a great pot of money has been dug up in the field, just behind Stuyvesant's orchard. Folks think it must have been buried there in old times by Peter Stuyvesant, the Dutch Governor.'

'Fudge!' said the one-eyed man of war, as he added a small portion of water to a bottom of brandy.

'Well, you may believe, or not, as you please,' said the host, somewhat annoyed, 'but everybody knows that the old governor buried a great deal of his money at the time of the Dutch troubles, when the English seized the province. They say, too, the old gentleman walks; aye, and in the very same clothes that he wears in the picture which hangs up in the family house.'

'Fudge!' said the half-pay officer.

'You may say "Fudge", but didn't Corney Van Zandt see him at midnight, stalking about in the meadow with his wooden leg, and a drawn sword in his hand, that flashed like fire? And what can he be walking for, but because people have been troubling the place where he buried his money in the old days?'

Here the landlord was interrupted by several guttural sounds from Ramm Rapelye, a sign that he was struggling with the unusual problem of having an idea. As he was too smart to insult so great a man, the host respectfully paused until Ramm had said his piece. Ramm's bulky frame now resembled a volcanic mountain on the point of an eruption. First, there was a certain heaving of the abdomen, not unlike an earthquake; then he emitted a cloud of tobacco smoke from the crater that was his mouth; then there was a kind of rattle in the throat, as if the idea were working its way up through a region of phlegm; eventually, his voice forced its way in the slow, but absolute tone of a man who feels the weight of his purse, if not of his ideas; his speech interspersed by a puff of tobacco smoke.

'Who talks of old Peter Stuyvesant's walking?—puff—Have people no respect for people?—puff—puff—Peter Stuyvesant knew better what to do with his money than to bury it—puff—I know the Stuyvesant family—puff—every one of them—puff—not a more respectable family in the province—puff—old standards—puff—warm householders—puff—none of your upstarts—puff—puff—puff. Don't talk to me of Peter Stuyvesant's walking—puff—puff—puff—puff.'

Here the redoubtable Ramm frowned, clasped up his mouth, and redoubled his smoking.

A general silence followed the sudden scolding of this very rich man. The subject, however, was too interesting to be readily abandoned. The conversation soon restarted from the lips of one of those narrative old men who seem to talk almost involuntarily.

Peechy Prauw Van Hook, the chronicler of the club, who could at any time tell as many stories in an evening as his listeners could digest in a month, now resumed the conversation, by affirming that, to his knowledge, money had at different times been dug up in various parts of the island. The lucky persons who had

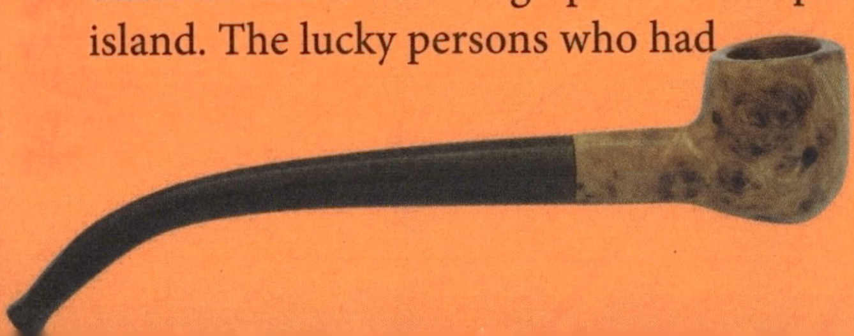

discovered them had always dreamt of treasure three times before they found it. He then pointed out categorically that these treasures had always been discovered by some descendant of the good old Dutch families, which clearly proved that they had been buried by Dutchmen in the olden time.

'Fiddle-stick with your Dutchmen!' cried the one-eyed captain. 'The Dutch had nothing to do with them. They were all buried by Kidd, the pirate, and his crew.'

This touched a chord that roused the whole company. The name of Captain Kidd was like a legend in those times, and was associated with a thousand marvellous stories.

The captain was a man of great weight among the peaceable members of the club, by reason of his military character, and of the gunpowder scenes which he said he had witnessed.

The golden stories of Kidd, however, were resolutely rivalled by the tales of Peechy Prauw, who—rather than allow his Dutch ancestors to be eclipsed by a crazy foreigner, enriched every spot in the neighbourhood with the hidden wealth of Peter Stuyvesant and his contemporaries.

Wolfert Webber had listened to the entire conversation. He returned home, his head full of magnificent ideas of buried riches. The soil of his native island seemed to have turned into gold dust; with every field teeming with treasure. His head almost reeled at the thought of how often he must have carelessly wandered over places where countless sums lay, just beneath the soil on which he trod. He was excited with this whirl of new ideas. As he came within view of his ancestral mansion, and the little realm where the Webbers had so long and so contentedly flourished, he railed against the narrowness of his destiny.

'Unlucky Wolfert!' he exclaimed, 'others can go to bed and dream themselves into whole mines of wealth; all they have to do is seize a spade in the morning, and turn up gold coins like potatoes, but you must dream of hardship, and rise to poverty—must dig your field from year's end to year's end, and—and yet raise nothing but cabbages!'

That night, Wolfert Webber went to bed with a heavy heart. The golden visions that disturbed his brain kept him up for hours and hours. The same visions, however, extended into his sleeping thoughts, and assumed a more definite form. He dreamt that he had discovered an immense treasure in the centre of his garden. At every stroke of

the spade he laid bare a golden ingot; diamond crosses sparkled out of the dust; bags of money, bulky with coins of silver or gold; and chests, wedged close with all kinds of gold coins, turned up their bellies, and yawned before his eyes, vomiting forth their glittering contents.

Wolfert awoke a poorer man than ever. He had no heart to go about his daily concerns, which appeared so trifling and worthless, but sat all day long in the chimney-corner, picturing ingots and heaps of gold in the fire. The next night, his dream was repeated. He was again in his garden, digging and laying open stores of hidden wealth. There was something very extraordinary in this repetition. He passed another day of reverie, and though it was cleaning day, and the house was completely topsy-turvy, he sat unmoved amidst the general uproar.

The third night, when he went to bed, his heart was pounding. He put on his red nightcap, inside-out for good luck. It was long past midnight before his anxious mind could settle itself into sleep. Again, the golden dream was repeated, and again he saw his garden teeming with ingots and moneybags.

Wolfert rose the next morning in complete bewilderment. A dream three times repeated was bound to come true and if so, his fortune was made.

In his agitation, he put on his waistcoat back to front—another sign of good luck. He no longer doubted that a huge store of money lay buried somewhere in his cabbage-field, shyly waiting to be sought for, and he rebuked himself for having spent his years in scratching about the surface of the soil, instead of digging to the centre.

He took his seat at the breakfast table full of these speculations. He was so absent-minded, that he asked his daughter to put a lump of gold into his tea instead of sugar, and begged his wife to help herself to a doubloon while handing her a plate of slap-jacks.

His greatest concern now was how to secure this immense treasure without anyone finding out about it. So, instead of working regularly in his grounds in the daytime, he now crept from his bed at night, and with spade and pickaxe, went to work to rip up and dig about his family's farm, from one end to the other. It did not take long before the whole garden—which had until recently look neat and tidy, with its phalanx of cabbages, like a vegetable army in battle formation—began to look like a scene of devastation. However, the persistent Wolfert went out each night, with nightcap on his head, armed with a lantern and spade in each hand. He continued to stalk through the slaughtered ranks, the destroying angel of his own vegetable-world.

Every morning bore testimony to the ravages of the preceding night in cabbages of all ages and conditions, from the tender sprout to the full-grown head, poorly rooted from their quiet beds like worthless weeds, and left to wither in the sunshine. It was in vain that Wolfert's wife protested; it was in vain his darling daughter wept over the destruction of her favourite marigolds.

'You shall have gold of another sort,' he would cry, chucking her under the chin, 'you shall have a string of crooked ducats for your wedding necklace, my child.'

His family began really to fear that the poor man was going out of his mind. He muttered in his sleep at night of mines of wealth, of pearls and diamonds and bars of gold. In the daytime, he was moody and distracted, and walked about as if in a trance. Dame Webber held frequent councils with all the old women of the neighbourhood; hardly an hour went by without one seeing wagging their white caps together round her door, while the poor woman made some piteous recital. The daughter, too, began to seek more frequent consolation from the stolen interviews with Dirk Waldron. She began to sing less and less frequently, and often forgot her sewing, to wistfully sit in her father's presence as he sat pondering by the fireside.

One day, Wolfert caught her eye fixed on him anxiously, and for a moment was roused from his golden reveries.

'Cheer up, my girl,' he said, with great elation. 'Why do you look so glum? You shall hold up your head one day with the Schermerhorns, the Van Hornes, and the Van Dams—the greatest landowners will be glad to get you for their sons!'

Amy shook her head at this vain-glorious boast, and worried about his mental health more than ever before.

In the meantime, Wolfert kept digging, but the field was extensive. And, as his dream had indicated no precise spot, he had to dig at random. The winter set in before one-tenth of the scene of promise had been explored. The ground became too frozen and the nights too cold to labour with a spade. So he stopped digging, but that was only temporary. As soon as the returning warmth of spring loosened the soil, and the small frogs begin to pipe in the meadows, Wolfert resumed his digging with renewed zeal. However, his working hours were reversed. Instead of working cheerily all day, planting and setting out his vegetables, he remained thoughtfully idle, until the shades of night summoned him to his secret labours. In this way, he continued to dig from night to night, and week to week, and month to month, but found nothing. On the contrary, the more he dug, the poorer he grew. The rich soil of his garden was dug away, and the sand and gravel from beneath were thrown to the surface, until the whole field looked like a sandy barrenness.

In the meantime, the seasons gradually rolled on. The little frogs that had piped in the meadows in early spring, croaked as bull-frogs in the brooks during the summer heat, and then sunk into silence. The peach tree budded, blossomed and bore its fruit. The swallows and martins came, twittered about the roof, built their nests, reared their young, held their congress along the eaves, and then winged their flight in search of another spring. The caterpillar spun its winding-sheet, dangled in it from the great buttonwood tree that shaded the house, turned into a moth, fluttered with the last sunshine of summer, and disappeared; and finally the leaves of the buttonwood tree turned yellow, then brown, then rustled one by one to the ground, and whirling about in little eddies of wind and dust, whispered that winter was at hand.

Wolfert gradually awoke from his dream of wealth as the year went on. He had not planted any crop to supply the wants of his household during winter. The season was long and severe, and for the first time the family had to give up some of its comforts. Gradually, reality stole into Wolfert's mind, and he realized that he was now poor, and that his family might go hungry. He already considered himself one of the most unfortunate men in the province, having lost such an incalculable amount of undiscovered treasure; so now—when thousands of pounds had eluded his search—it was cruel to have to be confused about shillings and pence.

More wrinkles formed on his brow, as he went about trying to earn money; his eyes bent downwards into the dust, with his hands in his pockets, as men are apt to do when they have nothing else to put into them. He could not even pass the city poorhouse without giving it a rueful glance, as if destined to be his future abode.

His neighbours began to comment on his strange conduct and unusual looks. For a long

time, they suspected he was crazy, and everybody pitied him; then, they began to suspect that he was poor, and then everybody avoided him.

His rich old friends met him outside their door when he went to visit, entertained him hospitably on the threshold, pressed him warmly by the hand on parting, shook their heads as he walked away, with the kind-hearted expression of 'poor Wolfert'. If they saw him approaching on the street, they quickly turned a corner and walked away. Even the barber and cobbler of the neighbourhood, and a tattered tailor in an alley hard by, three of the poorest and merriest rogues in the world, eyed him with that abundant sympathy which usually goes with a lack of means, and there is no a doubt that they would have loved to help him, if only they had any money.

Thus everybody deserted the Webber mansion, as if poverty was contagious, like the plague; everybody but honest Dirk Waldron, who still kept up his stolen visits to the daughter, and indeed seemed to grow more affectionate as the fortunes of his mistress continued to fall.

After some good counsel, Wolfert decided to lease the farm. As the people started coming and living there, the Webber family's prospects dramatically increased. The rent and the produce from the farm grown by the tenants, improved the financial prospects of the family. Thus, the

land ultimately produced the gold Worlfert was looking for.

After a few years, Dirk married Anna and lived happily in the mansion. The Webber mansion soon stood proudly as it once used to, and Wolfert took his rightful place on the armchair in the tavern, where he sat till the end of his life.

The Silver Skates

Mary Mapes Dodge

One bright December morning many years ago in Holland, two barely dressed children were seen on their knees on a bank of a frozen canal. The sun yet could not be seen, though its edges displayed the coming day.

The brother and sister were fastening something onto their feet, which certainly were not skates; they were pieces of wood that resembled skates!

They were the children of an impoverished peasant woman, who dare not even think about real skates for her two little ones! The children, nevertheless, spent many happy contended hours on the ice with these makeshift skates. The skates hurt their feet but they didn't mind the pain.

Suddenly a clear voice called out, 'Hans! Gretel!'

'It's mother,' Hans said and looked serious.

They pulled off their 'skates' and walked towards their cottage.

Their mother, tall and dressed in a petticoat, jacket and a tight cap, stood at the door, looking postcard picture of a Dutch village woman. Even if the cottage were a mile off, it would have seemed near. In the flat country of Holland, all objects stood out clearly in the distance. Dame Brinker and her youngsters knew this better than most.

Holland is a strange country, different from most others in the world. A large part of it is below sea level. Great dykes have been built to keep the ocean at bay. Sometimes these dykes leak, and disastrous results follow. Some of the keels of ships are taller than the rooftops!

Everywhere you can see ditches, ponds, canals, lakes and rivers. One may well ask, 'Is Holland the water or the shore?'

The children's father, Raff Brinker, had worked on the dykes for many years. When a flood threatened in a terrible storm, Raff fell from a scaffold and suffered severe head injuries. His wounds were so bad, he could never work again; he lost his memory but lived on, as an invalid.

Gretel only knew him as a peculiar silent man, although Hans had memories of a cheerful father who never tired of holding him on his shoulder and singing songs.

Dame Brinker supported her family by knitting, growing vegetables and spinning. She also did odd jobs on the canal boats to supplement her little earnings.

When Hans grew up to be a strong boy, he did all the drudgery. Also, since Raff's condition had worsened, he needed constant care.

Soon, by the time Hans was fifteen years old and Gretel, twelve, the two children were doing almost all the outdoor jobs—and the household work, too.

Hans and his sister were talented children. While he was good at wood carving, both of them were excellent gardeners. Gretel could also sing, sew and run on highstilts for miles. But she disliked books and Hans was steady but slow in his studies. He liked hard tasks—whether it was manual labour or studies.

While the children were helping their mother one December morning, a group of boys and girls came skating down the frozen canal. Among them were some fine skaters dressed in bright colourful costumes.

Hilda van Gleck, the daughter of the rich magistrate, was among them. She was wearing expensive furs and a loose-fitting sack. The others included an attractive peasant girl named Annie Bouman, the proud Rychie Korbes, daughter of the

famous actor Mynheer van Korbes, and a flock of others such as Peter and Ludwig van Holp, Jacob Poot, Carl Schummel and a small boy with a long name—Voostenwalbert Schimmelpenninck.

The youngsters skated all along the canal, displaying their racing prowess. People hurrying to work watched, as some of them glided—arms folded—under the very nose of a self-important doctor or law-giver! Or, a string of girls would suddenly halt when a fat magistrate was hurrying along to Amsterdam. The skates were beautiful indeed! They had superb strappings and shining runners and were topped with golden balls.

When they took a break, Rychie Korbes—who was their spokeswoman—announced, 'We are organizing a grand skating competition on the 20th, which is Meurouw van Gleck's birthday. The best skater will receive a splendid prize—a pair of lovely silver skates!'

'The girls' winner will get a pair with bells on it,' said Hilda, 'and the boys' prize will have an arrow carved on the two sides!'

At noon, Hans and Gretel went to practise on the canal.

Watching them, Carl Schummel said sarcastically to Hilda, 'A pretty duo of ragpickers!'

'The boy must have fashioned the skates himself,' Hilda said, softly.

Hilda went up to Gretel and asked her name.

'Gretel, Madam,' the child answered, awed by Hilda's high class. 'My brother's name is Hans.'

Hilda said, 'Join the skating competition. Entry is free.'

Hans replied, 'With our poor quality wooden skates, we will trip on the ice!'

Hilda spoke, 'Who is a better skater?'

Hans promptly replied, 'Gretel!'

And Gretel said, 'Hans!'

Hilda offered them money to buy skates but Hans said, 'We can't take the money,' and Hilda told him, 'Carve me a chain like the one Gretel is wearing; that will make you earn the money I give you.'

The next day, Hans Brinker was the proudest boy in Holland as he watched his sister sweep expertly among the other skaters. She was wearing a warm jacket that the kind Hilda had given her.

Peter van Holp exclaimed to Carl Schummel, 'That little girl skates well! It's like she has toes at the back of her feet and eyes in the back of her head! It will be funny if she enters the race and defeats Katrinka Flack!'

Christmas was approaching and Gretel was all dressed up and dancing for her mother and brother. But her father knew nothing. He sat with dull eyes as his daughter looked longingly at him.

They had a watch that belonged to their father and which the entire family cherished more than their life. It was a family heirloom that Dame Brinker would never give up—not even for gold or money to buy gifts for Christmas.

'For father's sake, we'll take care of it forever,' Hans said. 'Money may come to us when we don't even expect it.'

As Hans got ready to go to Amsterdam to buy her skates, Gretel began to sob.

'Allow me to remain back with you,' Gretel told her mother.

'Okay, but wait, Hans. I'll finish

making this pair of hose; sell it to the hosier and get us three quarter-guilders. We'll celebrate St Nicholas' Feast after all.'

Gretel was very happy. 'We too will be very merry like the rich people!'

Then Dame Brinker told them the story of St Nicholas: a cruel innkeeper once cut up three children and made them into pickle! St Nicholas came along and caught the wicked landlord. Then, he quickly turned the children back to their original selves—and that's why they celebrate the Feast of Saint Nicholas!

'Now go, Hans, and buy the skates.'

As Hans was on his way to Amsterdam, he saw coming towards him Dr Boekman, the most famous surgeon and physician in Holland! The doctor was a lanky man with stern blue eyes and compressed lips.

A voice whispered to Hans. 'God has sent you the greatest doctor in the land. How can you purchase skates when you can buy medical help for your father?'

Hans cried out, 'Mynheer Boekman!'

The great doctor stopped and scowled at the boy.

Hans panted and said, 'Mynheer, I wish to ask you a favour...'

The doctor muttered, 'I don't have any money...to give to beggars!'

'I am not a beggar, Mynheer,' Hans retorted proudly. 'I want your advice about my father. Though he lives, he can't think or speak coherently. He fell on his head on the dykes.'

The doctor started to listen to Hans's tale.

After completing the story, Hans told the doctor, 'Please see him, Mynheer. His mind is not well. I know the money I have with me is not enough. But I'll earn more. I will labour for you all my life, if you could only cure my father!'

Suddenly the doctor's face lit up.

'Keep your money. I will check your father.'

Then, the doctor asked him for more details about his father's condition. 'Ten years have passed—it's a terrible case. But expect me in a week's time. Where do you live?'

Hans told him.

The doctor muttered, 'I am happy with the boy…his eyes remind me of my poor Laurens's. I'll never forget that scoundrel!'

And so Hans went on and bought the skates.

Hans and his sister enjoyed themselves on the skates on the eve of St Nicholas' feast. Their mother was thrilled that the doctor would be visiting.

Hans was excited with the new skates, and impressed Gretel with many fancy displays on the ice. There were plenty of groups of skaters on the canal but the Brinkers did not care about them—though they were taunted by Carl Schummel, who bullied everyone.

At that moment, Jacob Poot approached them with a strange boy.

Carl exclaimed, 'Here's fatty! He's got a chap with him.'

Jacob made the introductions, 'This is my cousin, Benjamin Dobbs. He'll be in the race.'

It has been said that 'Old Nick'—St Nicholas or Santa Claus—originally came from Holland. But though he did, he changed over the years. In Holland, Saint Nicholas is quite literally a saint, and often comes in full formal dress—embroidered robes glittering with gold and gems, his crozier, mitre and jewelled gloves.

Also, in Holland, he visits the earth on the night of 5 December, hands out toys, candies and treasures to good children early the next morning, and then disappears for a year.

However, that night, St Nicholas did not visit the Brinker cottage! Why, you may ask. Well, I will tell you.

The night before St Nicolas's arrival, Herr Brinker got one of his fits. Since he had lost his mind, he never knew what he was doing. He caught hold of his wife and tried to push her into the fire. Fortunately, Dame Brinker survived the terrible ordeal but St Nicholas decided to skip their house.

On the day of the feast of St Nicholas, some of the boys from the school had decided to skate their way through parts of Holland. One of them had been carrying all their money, and suddenly discovered that the money was missing. They were a long, long way away from home! So they decided to turn back.

At the same time, Hans was heading to Leyden, to ask Dr Boekman to visit his father. Peter saw him and hailed him.

Hans's face brightened. 'Mynheer, it is good that we have met!'

'Can I help you?' Peter responded, cheerfully.

Hans replied, 'It is who can help Mynheer van Holp, by giving you this purse that I found!'

'Hurrah!' the boys shouted, after taking into their shivering hands the purse that contained their precious money.

Peter said, 'Thank you, Hans Brinker. How did you find the purse?'

'I was skating out of my house this morning, when I skidded against some lumber. As I was rubbing my hurt knee, I saw the purse under a log of wood.'

When Hans refused Peter's offer a reward for returning the money, Peter thought to himself, 'I like this boy.' Then, he asked Hans, 'What's your trouble?'

'I'm going to Leyden to see Dr Boekman, and don't have time to spare. Good day!'

'Wait,' Peter said, coming close to Hans. 'We are going to stop at Leyden anyway, so we can give your message to Dr Boekman.'

'But Hans,' he continued, 'Why go for Dr Boekman, Hans? There are others in Amsterdam who could help him, perhaps; he is a famous man, but he is a very expensive doctor, and he is also known to be a gruff man…'

'He promised, Mynheer, he promised me yesterday to come and see my father in a week; but now we think the poor father is dying. Oh! Mynheer, you can plead with him to come quick?'

'I will. However, the boys are very tired and cannot skate any more today. I promise to see the doctor early tomorrow, if he is in the city.'

Then the boys started off again.

The next day, Peter visited the hotel where Dr Boekman usually stayed whenever he came to

Leyden, but he had not arrived yet. So Peter asked his mother to send word to Hans Brinker that a letter with Hans's message had been given to the manager of the hotel to give to the doctor when he arrived.

After having a good look at some of the finest things that Holland has to show the world and a glimpse of the country's great history through its monuments, statues, cities and so on, the boys were on their way home!

Finally, they reached their hometown Broek! Katrinka was waiting on the canal! Carl was thrilled. Hilda was present! Peter felt at ease instantly. Jacob and Ludwig fell over each other in their enthusiasm to shake Katrinka's hands.

Annie thought, 'Where is Gretel?' Poor Gretel—how dreadful to have a father so dull and strange! Annie did not know about

his illness. No one usually paid much attention to Dame Brinker and her problems.

Annie Bouman was, indeed, the only one who felt no shame at being the friend of the Brinker siblings. She always got very angry when she heard people saying mean things about Gretel.

Gretel and Dame Brinker had not stirred since the fireside episode. Four days had passed and the group sat around the bed as sad as ever. Raff Brinker was paler than ever, though his fever had gone. But he did not know anything of what was happening around him. There was a second group of people in the room. Dr Boekman was speaking in low tones with a fat young man who listened keenly. The stout man was his assistant and student. Hans was there too. He stood respectfully at the window.

'Vollenhoven,' the doctor told his assistant, 'it clearly is a case of'—and here Dr Boekman began to speak in a mixture of Dutch and Latin medical terms that were quite untranslatable.

Vollenhoven looked on blankly as the great doctor spoke to him in easier phrases.

'It looks like the Rip Donderdunck case, when the man fell from the Voppelploot windmill. My learned colleague Von Choppem operated the man and found a dark sac that was pressing the brain. Choppem managed removed it. It was a great operation!'

'Mynheer, can you save this man?'

'Certainly,' the doctor stammered and then added, 'I hope so.'

The doctor then explained Raff Brinker's condition to Hans. He told to the boy what had to be done to save his father.

Hans listened carefully and looked anxiously at his father.

'The operation may kill father,' he commented.

'Yes, it may', the doctor replied, 'but I do believe that it will cure him.'

'I must talk to my mother alone,' Hans said.

Gretel became indignant and quickly walked away.

'Gretel, come back,' said Hans in sorrow.

Dame Brinker turned to Dr Boekman. 'Doctor, I give my consent.'

Dr Boekman got ready for the operation. He filled a basin full with water and kept it near the bed.

Then he asked Hans, 'Can you help me, boy?'

'Yes, I can.'

Gretel could not bear it. After peering from the crack of the door of the closet, she suddenly rushed across the house and ran away from the cottage.

During recess, the children from the nearby school gave a tremendous shout and rushed towards the canal! Children in colourful clothes skated gleefully and sang and screamed with laughter. They had locked up their Arithmetic, Latin and Grammar in the classroom.

At the height of the merriment, a child called out, 'What's that dark object near the idiot's cottage?'

A squeaky voice said, 'It's a bundle of rags.'

'It's Gretel, she's looking for rats!'

'Voost! You'll win a medal for your wit indeed!'

Gretel's mind was on other things, like the moans and noises that came from her cottage. Were they killing her father, she wondered.

Gretel shivered in the cold and cried bitterly.

Suddenly, she felt a firm hand on her shoulder.

'Get up, child,' a kind voice said.

Gretel raised her head and saw Hilda van Gleck who was looking at her with beautiful kind eyes. It was like a dream!

'Gretel Brinker! Wake up!' Hilda forced her to walk and Gretel felt better again.

After Gretel told Hilda about her father, the kind girl tried to peep into the house.

She called Gretel softly and said, 'Look, he's perhaps only asleep!'

Gretel got up and pressed her face to the window.

'My father is lying still. His head has a bandage. Everyone is staring at him,' Gretel screamed. 'I have to go to see my mother! Will you come?'

'The school bell has rung. I will return soon,' Hilda said.

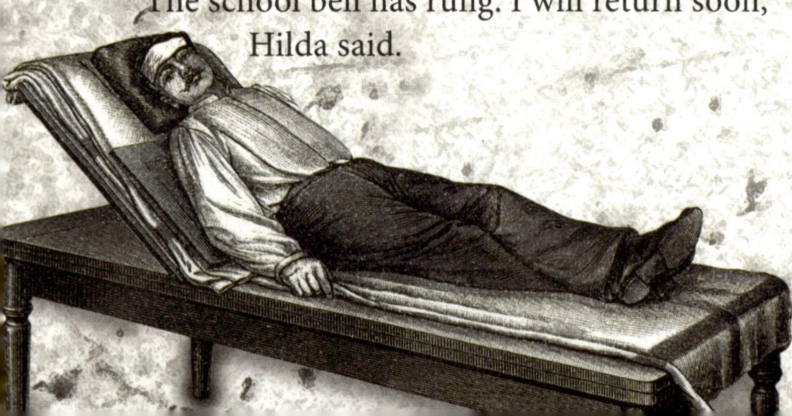

Gretel entered the house as silently as an angel! She went quietly to her mother. The room was so still that she could hear the doctor breathing. Her mother's hands were cold but her cheeks glowed. Her eyes were as bright as a deer's!

Dr Boekman leaned forward when the man on the bed started to move a bit. They were all startled!

The father's big hand, soft and white, twitched. It then moved towards his forehead, and felt the bandage in a questioning movement.

Dr Boekman held his breath as man's eyes slowly opened.

'Steady! Shift the mat higher! Throw on the clay...' Dame Brinker sprang like a young panther.

She seized her husband's hands and cried, 'Talk to me, Raff! Raff!'

'Meitje is it you?' he asked faintly. 'I was asleep and injured. Where is Hans?'

'I am here, father!' screamed Hans mad with joy.

Hans and Dame Brinker cried and laughed together, as they clung onto the newly awakened Raff. Gretel did not make a sound, but stared at all of them with happy startled eyes.

Her father spoke again, 'Is the baby asleep, Meitje?'

'The baby!' echoed Dame Brinker. 'Oh, Gretel! That is you! And he calls Hans, "Little Hans". Ten years asleep! Oh, Mynheer, you have saved us all. He has known nothing for ten years! Children, why don't you thank the meester?'

The good woman was beside herself with joy. Dr Boekman said nothing, but as his eye met hers, he pointed upwards. She understood. So did Hans and Gretel.

They all knelt by the bed and said a prayer of thanks to the Almighty. Dr Boekman bowed his head.

Gretel brought the Bible from the shelf and Dr Boekman—dismayed that Raff Brinker had called him a minister—handed the holy book to his assistant.

Hilda was scolded for returning to school late after recess. She had stayed near the cottage till she heard Dame Brinker cries of joy.

'I'm so glad, I'm so glad,' she said softly.

Peter was in an excellent state of mind the next morning, even though all the boys' bones ached due to their skating marathon. Hilda explained to him why Dame Brinker was laughing and was Hans was in a joyous mood. He didn't need further proof about Raff Brinker's near-miraculous cure.

The news, in fact, had spread in all directions. People who had never even cared for the Brinkers before or had never talked about them—except in a contemptuous manner or indifferently—were now unusually familiar with every detail of their story. There were also a huge number of rumours flying about.

Hilda's kind heart was flowing over. She paused to tell the tired doctor's coachman that she felt that the doctor would soon come out; she even she suspected that a most wonderful cure had occurred.

She tripped happily along the canal and resolved to tell all the children in school the story.

Janzoon Kolp, a local troublemaker, was skating by, and stopped when he came to the doctor's coach.

'Old man Brinker dead?' he asked, ignoring the coachman's disdainful stare.

The driver said nothing.

'See here, old pincushion, I'd run home and get you a chunk of gingerbread if I thought you could open your mouth,' Janzoon said, and repeated his question.

Suddenly the words came shooting out of the coachman's mouth, 'Not dead, he's cured!'

By the time the sun set, word had spread to the neighbouring towns that six men had to hold Brinker down as Dr Boekman poured huge amount of medicine into his throat. Brinker, the rumours said, had instantly jumped to his feet, all his faculties working well and began to talk like a lawyer! He had spoken

beautifully to his children and his wife Dame Brinker had hysterics laughing!

Dr Boekman visited the Brinker home and told the mother that her husband needed stronger nourishment. The cheerful aspect of the cottage soon disappeared when Dame Brinker thought how little money they had and it was impossible to feed Raff Brinker what the doctor recommended.

When Hans came home he said in alarm, 'What happened? Is the father still ill?'

She said, 'He is almost starving.'

Hans became pale.

'The doctor says he should have meat and wine. What will I do?' she sobbed.

Hans remained optimistic, 'Don't fear, mother; the worst is over. I'll find a job somewhere.'

Hans headed to the canal and was soon skating his way to Mynheer van Holp's house. But he turned back after thinking to himself, 'I cannot beg for money or food. I'll ask father if we can sell the watch—or pawn it.'

There was a surprise in store for him. His mother greeted him joyously and said, 'Hans! Hilda came here along with her maid. She has brought jelly, meat, wine and bread! Then the doctor sent his man with some more wine—and a nice bed as well as blankets for your father.'

'May God bless all of them!' echoed both the mother and son.

Raff Brinker soon regained his memory. He asked his family about old friends—one had died and the other was in jail, they told him. He insisted on sitting for sometime on the chair by the fireside.

Gretel ran about the place doing whatever she could to help her father. Hans stirred the fire and made it glow.

Later, after Raff Brinker ate well and went off to sleep, Hans and his mother sat talking. She told him how she and his father had saved over a thousand guilders, which disappeared overnight.

'One thousand guilders! What ever did become of them?' she said, 'If they went in an evil way, the thief would have confessed on his dying bed—he would not dare to die with such guilt on his soul!'

They heard Raff stir.

'Shhh,' she said to Hans. 'Don't say a word about it.'

Suddenly a faint voice spoke from the bed, 'The thousand guilders!' 'I had saved the money well. Did it last you all these years?'

But they did not want to tell him that not only had they not used the money, they hadn't even seen it!

Raff sensed something amiss and said, 'Didn't I tell you. I buried that money. I was injured and I did not trust Jan Kamphuisen. I'm glad he's now in jail. Only he and your mother knew that we had saved so much money.'

'I have not forgotten where I buried it. But for now, goodnight.'

Gretel then came forward and asked, 'Father, where did you hide the money?'

'Near the willow sapling at the back of our cottage,' Raff Brinker said in a drowsy voice. 'On the north side.'

Hans was ready to jump with joy as he wished his father goodnight!

Hans and Dame Brinker went out in the bright moonshine, carrying a spade and an implement to break ice. They saw clearly the willow tree. The ground was frozen and hard but the two were resolute.

With the help of the ice-breaker they managed to make an opening. After that the rest of the job was easy.

Hans was trembling and so was his mother. Their father had really dug deep! The hours passed and they kept on digging the hard earth.

Soon it would be daylight, but there was no money to be found!

Later in the morning Hans was hurrying down the road when he came across Annie Bouman.

'Good morning, Annie,' Hans said.

Annie smiled and wished him too.

'Annie, a great change has taken place at our house,' said Hans and went on to explain everything to Annie.

He added, 'I must hurry to Amsterdam to sell my skates. We need the money now and by evening I'll find a job.'

Annie was aghast!

'How can you sell your skates? The race is only five days away!'

'I know,' Hans answered. 'Bye!'

'Come back,' Annie shouted.

Hans spun around and returned to her.

'Hans, I know a person who will be happy to purchase your skates. Give the skates to me. I'll pay you the cash this afternoon!'

So Hans handed over the skates to the sweet girl.

Hans earned some money that day in Amsterdam helping a man with his loaded mules. But he failed to get a steady job anywhere. By sun down, Hans knew it was hopeless and he headed back home. He decided to go to the house of Mynheer van Holp. Fortunately for him, Peter was at home.

'Hans!' he cried, 'I wanted to meet you!'

He told Hans that he had work for him—working on the doors of the summerhouse in Haarlem immediately. He would have a comfortable workshop at his disposal. Peter had skated to Haarlem to arrange this idea with

Mynheer van Holp and he was happy to see young Brinker's glowing face!

Hans spoke briefly to Peter about Dr Boekman and then turned to leave. Peter did not have kind words for the 'gruff doctor'.

At that moment, a lady entered from an adjacent apartment. It was Mevrouw van Holp, dressed in a grandcap and long-laced satin aprons.

She said, 'I heard you and Peter speak about my friend Dr Boekman. He has a great sorrow. Many years back he lost his only son in painful circumstances. Before that tragedy, Dr Gerard Boekman was a very agreeable gentleman.'

Peter muttered something and then looked down as Hans put on his wooden skates.

'Why is he not wearing his new skates?' he asked himself but said nothing to Hans.

'I won't be entering the skating race, Mynheer,' Hans said and looked down.

'Why not?' Peter asked, and immediately suspected Carl Schummel of some foul play.

'Because I can't, Mynheer,' answered Hans.

As Hans came close to his house, he saw two figures moving about the doorway.

One was Gretel, dressed in her well-patched grey jacket, a blue skirt and a faded apron. The other was Annie! She was dressed in bright clothes and was wearing gold earrings.

'Hi! Girls, I've got work!'

His mother also had good tidings. Their father had sat up almost all day and was right now sleeping like a baby!

Then Annie said, 'I sold your skates; here's the cash.'

'Wow! Seven guilders!' cried Hans.

The children then ran after a rabbit that went to the back of their cottage. Annie made a pretty picture as she sat on a tree stump and posed.

'I will be your fairy godmother! I grant you two wishes,' she said playfully.

Hans said, 'I wish I'd find what I was looking for last night.'

Annie got up and stamped her foot thrice on the ground below her several times.

'Dig here before moonlight for hidden treasure!'

The Brinker children laughed at her.

Later, however, Hans brought the ice-breaker and started to dig near the tree stump.

'Mother! See!' suddenly Hans shouted.

'What's happened, boy?'

'Mother, this is the spot where the guilders are! The stump is that of the old tree you cut last year! It's the north side tree!'

Dame Brinker went down on her knees and saw Hans pull out an old pot made of stone! He put his hand in and pulled out an old bag—filled with guilders!

They laughed and cried in joy! There was such a noise as the money was counted. Raff Brinker smiled in his sleep.

The next day, Dr Boekman visited, to check on his patient, and Raff—who was regaining his memory with each passing day—partially resolved the story of the watch.

Ten years back he said, when he had rushed to the dykes when the waters were rising, he had met a young frightened boy who was running away.

'He caught my hand and handed me this watch. I never saw him again. But I never wanted to sell the watch for it didn't belong to me.'

Raff was then told the story of how they found the thousand guilders. They knew that such news would do him no harm. And it didn't. On the contrary, he shared their joy and happiness. Hans and his mother set out to enjoy the buying of provisions and peat!

After dinner, the watch affair was discussed again.

But before they could begin there was a knock on the door. It was Dr Boekman.

He said, 'I see that the patient is fast mending.'

'Mynheer,' cried the girl, 'He well may. For, last night, we discovered a thousand guilders that had been lost for a decade!'

Then suddenly Dame Brinker asked the doctor if he knew of a family called 'Boomphoffen.'

She then removed the watch from her pocket and showed it to the doctor.

'LJB!' Dr Boekman screamed in delight!

The Brinker family learned from the good doctor that the watch had belonged to his long lost son, who had also been his apprentice! The boy had accidentally poisoned one of his patients. And although no one blamed him for it, the boy believed he was to blame and ran away.

Since Raff's memory was not good enough to reveal where the doctor's son had gone, their visitor went away.

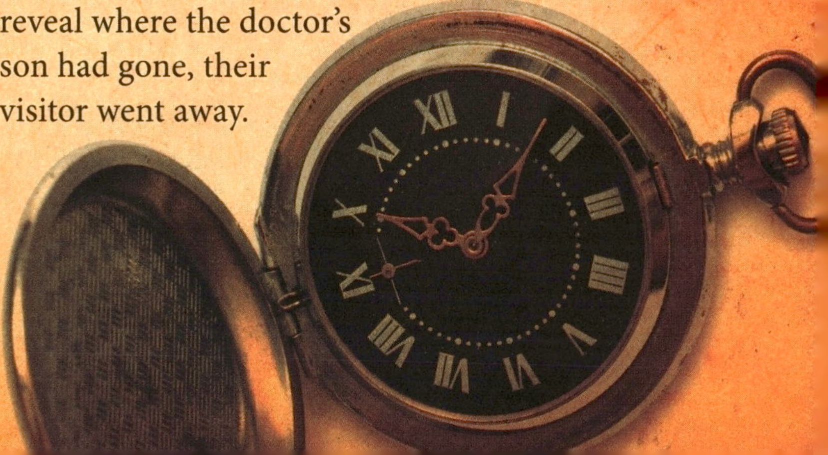

Soon, it was the day of the skating competition. A huge crowd had gathered around the venue. People dressed up in their best clothes thronged the place. It was truly a sight to watch!

The rules were simple: whoever won two races would be considered the winner.

Gretel won the first race, Hilda, the second, and then Gretel won the third, thus claiming the crown of 'Queen of Skating' and the silver skates.

Hans watched as Peter desperately tried to put his straps to prepare for the boys race. Peter said he would have to quit, as his straps were spoilt, but Hans said, 'Take mine…I have not practised for long and I don't have a chance of winning.'

Peter went on to win the boys' title. Hans thus returned the favour that Peter had done for him.

In the meantime, Raff Brinker remembered the name of the man with whom Laurens Boekman was living! It was a 'Thomas Higgs' who lived in Birmingham, England.

Arrangements were quickly made to bring the boy him home. It was a sight to watch when he met his father again after ten long years!

However, Laurens wanted to be a merchant, and shifted to Amsterdam.

The doctor then spoke to Hans.

'How old are you?'

'Fifteen, Mynheer,' said Hans.

'Would you like to study medicine and one day become my successor?'

'I would love to, Mynheer,' Hans replied happily.

And so, Hans grew up to become a doctor and married Annie.

But what of dear, quick, patient little Gretel? Well, she grew up to become an amazing singer, a fabulous sister, a sweet little wife, while remaining, as she was, a delightful daughter. Her neighbours, however, will always remember her as the little girl who won the Silver Skates.

The Phoenix and the Carpet

Edith Nesbit

It was nearly the fifth of November and there was scepticism about the quality of the fireworks that were purchased for the Guy Fawkes festivities.

I think it was Robert who said, 'They are cheap. What if they don't go off? That'll give the Prosser kids plenty to snigger about.'

Jane said, 'The crackers I bought are fine. The shopkeeper told me they were worth thribble their price—'.

'Thribble is not grammar,' Anthea said and Cyril agreed.

'It isn't grammar,' he said. 'One word is not grammar.'

Anthea was thinking of a very nasty answer, but she remembered how the boys were disappointed because they could not get to ride on the tram to London. Their mother had promised them the ride if they remembered to wipe their shoes on the rug for six straight days when they returned from school. However, because of the wet days, they could not keep that resolution.

So Anthea just said, 'Squirrel, don't be too clever. The fireworks are fine, you'll get the eight pence tram fares that were not bought today, to purchase something else with it. You should get a lovely Catharine wheel for that money.'

Cyril coldly said, 'It's not your eight pence anyway.' Cyril's nickname was 'Squirrel', just as Anthea's was 'Panther'.

Robert said, 'Think of the fireworks. We must not look foolish in front of the kids next door. I think we should test them.'

'Duffer,' Cyril said. 'Fireworks can be used only once!'

Nevertheless, they decided to test the fireworks, which were placed on the table and the four kids closed their eyes and grasped something. Robert got a cracker, Anthea and Cyril, Roman candles and little Jane's fat hand claimed the jewel in the collection—the jack-in-the-box, which cost two shillings.

The Roman candles and the cracker were lit and they were what you would have expected. But the jack-in-the-box just sat in its tray and laughed at the children, as Cyril described it. They tried matches, paper and Vesuvian matchsticks from father's overcoat pocket—but to no avail. Anthea then went to the cupboard below the stairs and brought some paraffin from there.

Just when Cyril was lighting the twenty-third match to the jack-in-the-box, Anthea flung the paraffin on the tray. The jack-in-the-box didn't catch fire—but the paraffin surely did act differently. A flash of hot flame flew up and scorched Cyril's eyelashes and the faces of all the children before they could react.

As they backed off, the flame touched the ceiling.

The flame quickly spread and Robert and Cyril knew there was little time to be wasted. They lifted the carpet and kicked it over the tray. This stopped the fire and only smoke, and a dreadful smell, remained.

But suddenly the jack-in-the-box began to act for it had been lit at last. It roared beneath the carpet in all its fury! It went on, bursting and banging and spluttering even below the table.

Anthea's howls brought mother rushing in. After a few moments the cracker fizzled out and there was a deadly silence all around. The children looked at each other's blackened faces—and at their mother's white face.

The children's parents took possession of the remaining fireworks and mother was unhappy when father himself let them off in the garden at the back—a sight which the children enjoyed from the windows of their bedrooms.

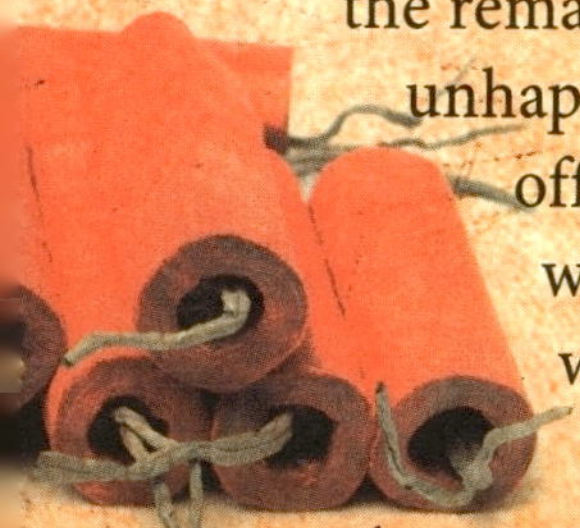

All was forgiven the next day, when a man came at tea time with a rolled up carpet.

Mother said, 'If it isn't in good shape, you'll have to exchange it,' and the man reassured her of its quality.

When the carpet was unrolled in the nursery, something hard fell out and rolled on the floor! The children scrambled after it and Cyril grabbed it. It was egg-shaped, shiny and yellow and partially transparent. It radiated an odd kind of light that changed when it was held in different ways. It looked like an egg with a fiery yolk that just glimmered through the stone!

Mother told the children they couldn't keep it; they had to return it to the man who had brought the carpet.

So the children trooped off to the man's shop. As soon as he saw the kids, he recognized them and started talking in a loud voice.

'I'm not taking back the carpet. A bargain is a bargain!'

The children began to explain the egg phenomenon but the man wouldn't listen.

When Jane said, 'There was an egg,' the man rushed at them and the children fled the spot.

The egg was now theirs and was thus placed on the mantelpiece. It brightened up the rather dull and dark nursery.

On Guy Fawkes Day, mother and father went to the cinema. The children were unhappy, for the Prossers were having fun with a plenty of fireworks next door, while they didn't have any. They weren't even allowed a bonfire in their garden.

After their baby brother—who was called 'the Lamb', because the first thing he ever said was 'Baa!'—had been put to bed, they sat mournfully round the nursery fire.

Anthea tried to raise their spirits by saying, 'Think about our last holidays!'

On their previous holidays they had found a Psammead, a sand fairy, who allowed them anything that they wished for.

To pass the time, they waved tablecloths at the 'magic' tracings they had made on the carpet but nothing happened. Robert's cloth struck the golden egg which rolled under the fire grill. Robert took hold of the egg. It was so hot that he dropped it immediately. It bounced right into the flames.

The red, hot egg suddenly cracked in two and a colourful bird came out of it. In front of the children's eyes the flame-coloured wings began to grow larger and larger! They stared at it, their eyes and mouths wide open.

The bird rose from its fiery nest and flew about the room and finally sat on the fender. It moved its head to one side like a parrot and the children were not surprised when it said, 'Take care, I haven't cooled down yet.'

The children stared at the bird, whose feathers looked like gold.

The bird asked, 'Who placed the egg in the flame?'

When three fingers indicated it was Robert, the bird told Robert in a well-bred tone, 'I am indebted to you.'

The bird was happy when Robert said, 'You're the Phoenix.'

Robert had found a book with pictures of the Phoenix.

Cyril fetched an encyclopedia which had the description of the bird: 'Phoenix, a magnificent bird of antiquity.'

The Phoenix then told them its story.

'I live for 500 years and then burn myself and my egg hatches into a new Phoenix. It had become a bad habit that I could not break. One day a princess and a prince flew on a magic carpet to live their lives alone away from everything—they loved each other so much. Since they had no use for the magic carpet, they gave it to me. And that is the carpet,' the bird said, pointing its beak to the carpet that mother had bought for twenty-two shillings, nine pence!

At that moment they heard father opening the door.

'Make two wishes,' said the Phoenix, 'one to get into bed instantly and the other for the carpet to get back to its proper place.'

This was done and kids were in bed in an instant, the lights out.

The next morning Jane asked the bird, 'Can you grant us wishes?'

'No, not me,' the Phoenix answered her.

As someone's footsteps were heard, the Phoenix quickly hid itself.

When they were free from their studies and chores, the children locked all the doors and windows, moved the chairs and table from the carpet and Anthea cleaned it.

Then they dressed in their outdoor clothes, for they didn't really know where they would be going.

Robert roused the Phoenix who let him lift it to the carpet, where it immediately fell asleep again. Everyone then sat on the carpet and asked each other where they would go.

They awakened the Phoenix who said, 'Let the carpet decide!'

They responded, 'We wish to go abroad.'

They did, and in a moment their world appeared to turn upside down. When it became right, they were outdoors—and up, up and away!

Soon, they were floating safely and splendidly in the clear air, blues skies above them, the azure sea far below.

'We are above the French coast,' the Phoenix announced. 'Where do you want to go? I'll keep one wish for emergencies.'

Incidentally, the children were allowed only three wishes a day.

Jane said, 'It's the size of our carpet. Let's land there. We can get out to buy food from there.' Anthea had started to suggest something else when Jane complained that just because she was the youngest her suggestions were not listened to. So she said, 'I wish our carpet would settle on the top of the tower!'

And the carpet did just that!

But the tower was hollow at the top and the children soon found themselves sinking to the bottom. Seeing an owl's nest pass by, Robert put his hand out to get some eggs and soon found himself stranded on the tower's ledge outside the carpet! By the time he had turned around the carpet had sunk some thirty feet. Robert was stuck!

The feelings of his siblings sunk to its lowest, as the carpet descended to the tower's bottom.

Then Cyril said, 'We can't leave Robert there. I wish our carpet would get him down.'

And the carpet awoke! It pulled itself together and floated upwards and settled on the uneven floor where Robert soon took refuge.

'Oh, that was close!' said Robert. Let's wish we were at home eating mutton and jam!'

But this time the carpet didn't budge. They had finished their three wishes for the day. The Phoenix was fast asleep. Anthea woke the bird.

'How will we get home?' asked Cyril.

'I have no idea,' the Phoenix replied. 'But I'll get you something to eat.' And it fluttered up the tower's grey space and vanished.

When it returned the children saw that it was carrying a basket full of boiled chestnuts, a piece of bread and a very big pear in its beak. They all felt better after eating, but how to return home?

The Phoenix told them, 'I'll do my best to get you home. I can help you but it will take an hour or two.'

When the Phoenix took off again, the restless children found a small dark space after dislodging some stones near them. They explored it and came upon a door and when they peeped inside they saw that it was pitch dark. Nevertheless, they entered the cave and lit matches to find their way about. They discovered that it was a sort of tunnel and dislodged more stones so that they could search the place better.

Robert said, 'This is the place where you'll find buried treasure.'

And so they proceeded forward and down seventeen steps. He found something and his hand touched a bag that contained what seemed to be marbles.

'Buried treasure!' he cried.

When he snatched the bag, it gave way and gold coins tumbled out of it and rolled on the floor! Then his last matchstick got over.

'Let's get out,' he said when all of a sudden they felt a whirring sound like an earthquake—and they were back in the breakfast-room at their home.

How bright and safe the place seemed! The Phoenix stood on the mantelpiece, waiting to be thanked.

In reply to their question, he said, 'Oh, I simply went to your pal the Psammead and got a wish from it.'

'The carpet told me where to find the Psammead; you know these wishing things know everything about one another.'

It started when the cook gave notice on Sunday because she said that the carpet was too dirty with foreign mud to be cleaned.

The children were asked to explain the carpet's muddiness and as they got into a twist trying to do so—their tale of the tower and the treasure was met with such disbelief by their parents that they were forbidden from using the carpet till Saturday.

Saturday came along with the carpet—and the Phoenix who was found beneath the table perched on a bar of wood.

They were talking things over when the cook burst into the room, holding a broken basin.

'It's the only basin I have; how will I make the kidney pudding and beefsteak?'

A lot of arguments ensued between the children and the cook who also asked them where they got the 'yellow fowl'.

Anthea said suddenly, 'I wish, we were on a sun-kissed southern shore!'

And her wish was granted, the cook and the Lamb also getting transported to that sunny destination.

The island was inhabited by savages who wanted a cook! They believed she was the queen they were promised they would get—her white cap was mistaken for a crown!

They put wreaths around her neck and began to dance around her. The 'queen' clapped wildly and shouted, 'Bravo!'

The children decided to return home without a cook and the magic carpet transported them back.

On Monday morning, Anthea felt that the cook should be brought back and so she sat on the carpet and asked it to take her back to the southern shore. But when she encountered the cook, the latter seemed very much at home as queen of the savages.

Anthea decided to tell her mother the whole truth, which the Phoenix said was a good idea but one which Anthea would not be able to carry out. And the golden bird was right! Hardly did Anthea start telling mother about the magic carpet rides and the Phoenix that her mother cut her off.

When Anthea said that the carpet took them wherever they wanted, mother replied, 'It would be nice if it could take you some place where you could get some Eastern stuff for my bazaar.'

Mother took the Lamb with her to Bournemouth, father went to Scotland on work and the Phoenix asked to be left alone for one week.

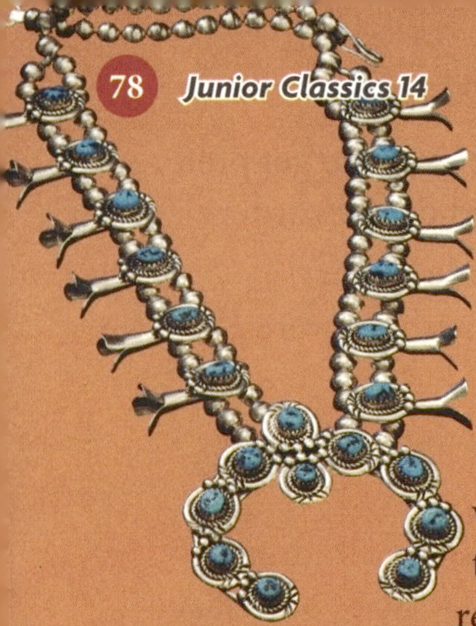

The children thought about their next journey.

Anthea said, 'Mother told me she wanted Indian stuff for her bazaar.'

So on Saturday they went off to the East after telling the carpet, 'We require Indian things for the bazaar. Please take us there.'

And the carpet swirled away till they landed near an Indian town. The roofs and domes—and a man on an elephant besides two English soldiers—confirmed that it was India.

'We must meet a raja,' said Jane.

Just then a man approached them, bowed and said, 'My queen thinks you are very good children. Come and meet her.'

So they went to the palace and met the old queen. She wanted to buy their carpet but they said they could not sell it. Instead they told her their story—all of it. The queen and her courtiers enjoyed their tale very much. Then the children asked the queen where they could get Indian goods for their mother's bazaar. The queen gave them her turquoise necklace! That, of course, wouldn't do for a mere bazaar and they told her that.

So the queen sent her servants to get pretty little things which were piled on the carpet.

Before leaving, Cyril made a short farewell speech and said, 'I wish we were at the school's bazaar!'

And they were there, leaving the queen courtiers dumbfounded!

The carpet had deposited the children in a space between two stalls. All types of bazaar things lay on the floor.

The children slowly crawled out but soon Robert got into a quarrel with Mrs Biddle, who ran the stall. She had accidentally walked on his hand and when he yelled out in pain and a crowd gathered, Mrs Biddle scolded him!

Miss Peasmarsh, who ran the other, adjoining stall, rather liked the children, which upset Mrs Biddle some more.

When the Indian things were discovered, these two ladies began squabbling about their ownership. The children settled the issue by writing a short note on a blue paper which read, 'Those pretty Indian things are for Miss Peasmarsh's stall.'

Mrs Biddle made an appeal to the bazaar committee, but the blue paper was discovered, and Miss Peasmarsh got all the things. She sold them for a total of thirty-five pounds.

The kids discovered later that Miss Peasmarsh had also sold the carpet! That too, to Mrs Biddle!

The children felt miserable. They did not lose their good manners, however, and spoke graciously to everyone at the bazaar before leaving.

They decided to approach Mrs Biddle directly and were soon knocking at her door. When the door was opened Anthea walked past an uncomfortable parlour maid, the others following her. Mrs Biddle was straightening out the carpet with the very boot that had stomped on Robert's hand. She suddenly turned around and saw her visitors.

Her face turned a dark violet.

'You wicked things!' she cried, 'go away, or I'll call the police.'

Mrs Biddle kept on raving and ranting at them so Anthea did what she thought was best for them.

She said, 'I wish Mrs Biddle's mood changes into an angelic good temper!'

And Mrs Biddle's face rapidly changed colour—from purple to violet to mauve to pink! And she then had a jolly smile!

The carpet had accomplished another feat.

Cyril said, 'I'm sorry we angered you at the bazaar.'

'Don't say a word,' said the transformed Mrs Biddle. 'You can have the carpet of course, my dears. And I take no more than the ten shillings I paid for it.'

Two days later, Cyril was wondering where the Phoenix was. Anthea looked under the chairs and tables, in baskets and boxes in father's suitcase and mother's work bag but the bird was nowhere to be found.

Then Robert suddenly said, 'You beautiful old Phoenix, come along,' and immediately the Phoenix came sailing into the room.

'Let's not use the carpet. Let's do something different. I want to go to one of my temples in the city,' the Phoenix declared.

'The fire insurance office?' asked Robert. 'It's not actually a temple.'

But the bird said coldly, 'It is a temple.'

The tram was the best way to get to the 'temple'. It was a lovely ride and the children felt lucky they had the money to pay for the tickets.

Soon, they reached a huge house in Lombard Street where the Phoenix's image was carved in stone. On polished brass were the words: Phoenix Fire Office.

The Phoenix told the children, 'Tell them we want to meet the High Priest. Tell them to take you to the sacred sanctuary.'

The children trooped in and first encountered an attentive clerk dressed in black.

He asked them, 'What do you children want?'

When they replied, 'We want to meet the High Priest,' he brushed them off, but another gentleman came in.

The delightful gentleman wore a beard and had merry and kind eyes. Despite this, it was hard for them to explain things.

'What can I do for you?' he asked.

'We'd like to talk to you in private,' said Robert so they were taken to a room upstairs.

There the gentleman told them, 'Tell me what you need.'

'You have named your establishment after the Phoenix,' Cyril said, 'but did you know there is a real Phoenix. It's buttoned up against Robert's chest!'

'Goodness gracious!' the gentleman exclaimed, when he set his eyes on the Phoenix! And he jumped when the bird started to talk!

The Phoenix said, 'I am the head of your house. I have come here to accept your homage.'

Since the manager was absent, the nice gentleman made all the employees come up and take a look, one by one, at the 'head of the house'.

Then a ceremony was organized in the board room where all the staff members paid their respects to the Phoenix.

Then all the employees returned to their respective work stations; no one talked about what had just taken place. They did not even look at each other, as if what they just experienced was only a dream!

The Phoenix however, was very happy and wrote an ode to itself.

The children's next wish was to do a kind and good deed. So, they sat on the carpet and wished. But after the usual swirling, they found themselves landing in their own house!

Robert then said, 'We don't want to do good work in our own house—we want to do them somewhere else.'

The willing carpet began its work and the children and bird crashed in a heap of complete darkness.

Robert had a match and soon they could see that they were in a kind of dungeon. Suddenly Robert's leg touched an old bag. When they checked it out, they saw that it contained gold coins.

'We cannot take that money, it's not ours,' Anthea said, although Cyril felt they could take it and spend it on the poor.

Finally, they decided to stop arguing and to find their way out. They had to break an ancient trap door that was stuck tight, but eventually saw last saw blue skies and the green countryside!

They knocked on the door of a small house and were greeted by a lady who spoke broken English and French. As she spoke to them, the lady began to weep.

Anthea said, 'We are sorry, but we only came here to enquire about the castle on the hill.'

Calling Anthea an 'angel', the poor lady said, 'That castle was ours but tomorrow we are going to sell it to strangers. My brother, the Marquis, has spent all his money and we have no choice but to sell.'

'What would you feel if you found hundreds of thousands of gold pieces?' Cyril asked the lady.

The lady allowed herself a sad smile and said, 'Oh! You have heard the legend? It is only an account by the fairies.'

When the children told her that they had actually seen it, she said that first should talk to the curate. That gentleman too was sceptical but finally they all decided to go to the place where the children had seen the treasure.

The curate and the lady hugged each other in joy as tears streamed down their faces when they were shown the treasure.

The Phoenix told them to make a fast exit. So they went to their carpet and were soon discussing the good deed they had done, sitting in the comfort of their nursery at home.

For their next adventure, the children felt they should try something new. They would not go out, they'd ask the carpet to bring something in.

So they wrote a note that said, 'We want you to bring the loveliest productions from your native land', signed it, and pinned it to the carpet.

So off the carpet went—and returned with 199 Persian cats! It was a Persian carpet after all!

'How do we feed them?' the children asked each other.

So they shot off another request to the carpet—which zoomed off and returned with 398 rats!

The noise this gathering made caused a policeman to come to the house and demand what was going on. He wanted to inspect all the rooms, to see if any cats were being 'ill-treated'.

Fortunately for the children, at that moment screams from the street rent the air, 'Murder, murder, stop thief!' The policeman had no choice but to stop his inspection of the house and look into the more serious matter of a murderer-thief.

Cyril, meanwhile, wrote the note that directed the carpet to take the rats away and bring some milk for the cats. The carpet got rid of the rats, but brought back a Jersey cow for the milk!

None of them could milk a cow and again they were in a dilemma. Since their parents were away on holiday, they could stay awake till late but at one o' clock in the morning they were too tired to stand and they decided to get to bed and leave the cats to themselves.

Jane suddenly awoke and heard the muffled sound of someone walking about the house. When she investigated the matter, she saw that it wasn't her brothers but a burglar!

Jane did not run away or scream, as you would think! Instead she began a conversation with the robber.

As she approached him the burglar suddenly breathed deeply and spoke.

'It's judgement,' he said. 'Cats and more cats! I don't mind the cow. She's fine!'

'Send for the police, I'll go quietly,' he told Jane who told him that it wasn't a dream and that the cats were real.

Jane was soon joined by the others. They asked the burglar if he would milk the cow, for he had shown a certain liking for that animal.

'Sure I could,' he replied.

And the children brought saucepans and bowls and all kinds of utensils that could hold milk and the burglar started the milking. He was good in this job and soon there was enough milk for the cats.

After they had talked for a while, Jane asked the burglar, 'Will you take the cats away? They'll fetch you good money.'

'I'll get a pal to haul them off,' he said and returned as promised with a fellow burglar, sacks and a cart. Soon the cats were dispatched by these two men and peace descended on the house.

The carpet was told to take the cow away and return itself to the nursery floor, which it did.

The next day the children got some unexpected bad news. The burglar who had taken the cats from them had been arrested by the police on charges of stealing the cats. So, the kids decided to rescue the burglar and landed in his cell via the carpet.

'How would you like to go a southern island where you can live in comfort and not do any work?'

The idea appealed to the thief—the children planned to set him up with the cook—and soon they were flying again to the southern isle where the cook was the queen.

'I wish we were all on the sunny southern shore where the cook is.'

And they were! The burglar found the cook to be a pleasant companion, but there was a hitch. She would only get married to him if a clergyman performed the ceremony. So the children wished for that and the carpet brought a clergyman to the island, who married the couple. After the wedding, they all had a big feast!

The children wanted to buy a gift for their mother but did not know how to wish for it. Jane hit on an idea.

'We'll tell the carpet to take us to a place where we'll get the money for the gift—in a way that isn't wrong.'

So the words were spoken and they were on the move. By this time, already tatty, the carpet had a lot many holes thanks to the rats. The children had not mended it properly. As a result, some of the darning gave way with the children's weight, and Robert and Jane slipped through the hole while still in the air. They landed on the roof of a big house in New Cross.

The carpet kept moving and sank quickly on the pavement at Deptford Road. The other children heard a familiar voice shout, 'Well, what are you doing here?'

It was their favourite uncle—Uncle Reginald.

'We were going to Greenwich Palace...' said Cyril.

'Where are the others?' Uncle Reginald asked. 'Anyway, I must rush. I've got a case to attend to. That's the worst of being a solicitor.'

Then he took out some money from his pocket and gave it to the children. It was a gold sovereign!

The children were overjoyed.

Meanwhile Robert and Jane were trying to open a trap door on the terrace where they landed. When it opened, they peeped inside and heard a voice screaming.

They were discovered!

'Where's the rest of your thieves?' the screaming lady asked.

Then she called out, 'Septimus!'

Fortunately for the children, Septimus was the clergyman who had married the cook and he listened to them patiently when they told him their tale. And while they were standing in front of him—the Phoenix came to their rescue. He had asked the Psammead for a wish and that was granted. The two children were soon safe in their nursery at home.

There was a joyful reunion and then they went out and bought mother's gifts—two white and blue vases, one pink silk handkerchief, a bottle of

perfume, a cake of soap and a box of Christmas candles.

Now, we have come near the end of our story but before we go, we must tell you how Baby Lamb disappeared!

One evening the children were playing with Baby Lamb in their nursery when suddenly, after Lamb muttered some baby words, he and the carpet disappeared! The baby had been flown away on a magic carpet full of holes!

Jane started crying and Anthea was frantic and pale.

The Phoenix had the answer to the baby's disappearance.

'It must have made a wish … the carpet understands all languages—.'

And the bird was right. At that terrible moment, their mother rang her bell. She had been ill, and was resting. Anthea went to her mother's room.

Mother began to speak, 'The Lamb'.

Anthea tried to explain but mother went on.

'Lamb was very good at first, but he's pulled the toilet-cover off the dressing table with all the brushes and pots and things... Now he's become so quiet I'm afraid he's up to more mischief. Could you check on him?'

'He's here?!' an astonished Anthea asked.

'Of course,' said mother impatiently.

Anthea looked around. There was no Lamb. She returned to the nursery to find Lamb playing on the carpet, and surrounded by his siblings!

The Phoenix explained that 'Aggety dag', the nonsense word that Lamb had been saying earlier meant, 'I want to be with my mother,' in baby language.

'And the carpet understands all languages!'

The bird added, 'He came back to the nursery because I went to the Psammead and wished that Lamb were restored to you.'

Two days later, coconut matting replaced the torn carpet. The children also did not want the Phoenix to stay longer but they could not tell it to its face.

'What will happen to the magic carpet?' it asked.

Anthea replied, 'The ragman will take it away tomorrow.'

The Phoenix made a small speech, 'I will not break the news gently. I must leave you now.'

All the children sighed in relief.

'Must you go so soon?' Anthea murmured.

'I really must, dear,' replied the Phoenix. 'I ask for one last request. Give me the torn carpet.'

'We will,' said Robert.

The Phoenix now wanted the last rites to be performed so that it could lay its egg and burst into flames. When the children left the room to get the materials for the pyre—sandalwood, incense and other stuff—the Phoenix laid its egg.

'Send a note to the Psammead to take the egg away and keep it for another 2,000 years,' the Phoenix said.

Soon, a fire was lit and the bird had burst into flames, its 'goodbyes' slowly faded away. All the children cried bitterly.

That same night, a huge box was delivered to their home. When the children opened the box, they found it contained all that the kids had always cherished: games, toys and books, candied cherries and chocolate, cameras and paintboxes—plus all the gifts they had wanted to give to their parents and Lamb.

At the bottom of the container was a small golden feather. And pinned to a beautiful fur cloak meant for mother, was a paper which said, 'With gratitude, in return for the carpet—P.'

The Little Prince

Antoine de Saint-Exupéry

When I was six years old, I came across a book that showed a picture of a boa constrictor swallowing an animal. The book also said that boa constrictors swallowed their prey whole and slept for six months while they digested their food.

Inspired, I drew my first picture of a boa constrictor eating an elephant. But the adults who saw the drawing thought it was a hat. I drew another picture; this time, I showed the whole elephant inside the boa constrictor. However, I still had to explain it to the adults; and then they told me to give up drawing and focus instead on geography, history, mathematics and grammar.

Thus, at age six, I gave up becoming a painter. I grew up and became an airplane pilot. I have to admit, though, that geography did help me distinguish between China and Arizona.

In the course of this life, I have encountered several people. Some people seemed to be properly clear-headed; but when I showed them my drawing of the boa constrictor and the elephant, they always thought it was a drawing of a hat.

Once this happened, I would never speak to them again about boa constrictors. Instead, I would come down to their level and talk to them about golf, and politics and bridge. And the grown-ups would be very pleased to have met someone sensible.

Thus, I lived my life alone with no one to really talk to until my plane accident in the Sahara six years ago. As I had no one with me, I set out to do the repairs myself. It was a matter of life and death: the water I had would hardly last me a week!

That first night, I slept on the sand, far, far away from any human habitation. Which is why I was shocked to be woken up at sunrise by a voice asking me to draw a sheep.

'What?' I asked.

'Draw me a sheep!'

Jumping to my feet, I blinked hard; and saw the most extraordinary little person looking at me with utmost seriousness.

Much later, I sketched a portrait of the boy, with is the best likeness of him that I could draw—as I was discouraged to pursue a career in painting, I could not make this drawing of him as charming as the person himself.

You have to remember, I had crashed far, far away from human habitation and so I was a bit unsure of this child lost in the desert, even though he did not look like he was lost.

He stared at me gravely and asked again, 'If you please, draw me a sheep.'

When I could finally find some words, I told him I didn't know how to draw.

'That doesn't matter. Draw me a sheep,' he replied.

So, I took out my sheet of paper and fountain pen and drew one of the only two pictures I had ever learnt to draw.

Imagine my surprise when the stranger in the desert promptly looked at the drawing and said, 'No, I don't want an elephant inside a boa constrictor. What I need is a sheep. Draw me a sheep.'

So I drew him a sheep.

But the small person found it too sickly. I drew another one, he rejected that as well. I drew a third, and he didn't like that either. Finally, when I had run out of patience, as I wanted to get to the faulty engine of my plane, I drew one last picture and gave him an explanation to go with it.

'This is just his box. The sheep you want is inside.'

To my surprise, my young judge was quite happy with it and told me, 'This is exactly the way I want it.'

His only concern was whether the sheep would require a lot of grass to eat and I assured him that the sheep would have enough grass as it was very small.

This is how I met the little prince.

For all his curiosity about me and my plane, the little prince did not say much about himself. I got to learn about him through off-hand comments.

For example, when I told him my plane could fly, the little prince asked me, 'So, you too come from the sky. Which is your planet?'

Thus, I found out that he came from another planet. But when I asked him where he was from, he fell silent.

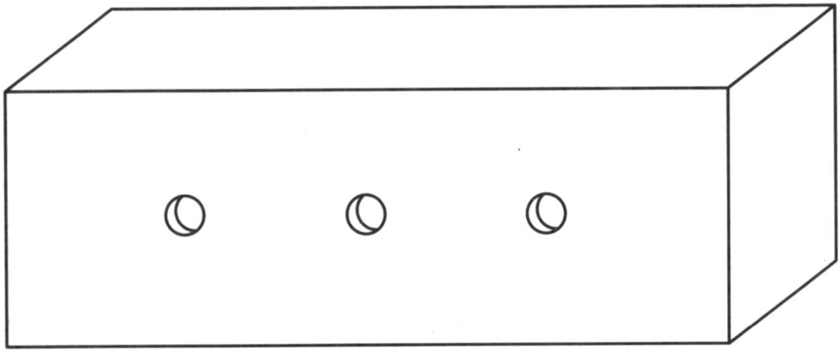

So, I asked him where he wanted to take the sheep. After a reflective silence, the little prince said, 'The best thing about this box that you have given me is that the sheep can use it as a house at night.'

But when I offered him string and a post, so he could tie up the sheep during the day, the prince just laughed.

'Tie him up! What a strange idea!'

He told me there was no need to tie the sheep as he didn't have very far to go.

Thus, I learnt that the little prince came from a place which was hardly bigger than a house.

But it came as no surprise. I knew that apart from the Earth, Mars, Venus, Jupiter there were hundreds of other planets—some so small they were hard to see through a telescope. In fact, astronomers who discover such a planet give it a number, not a name.

I strongly believe that the planet the little prince came from is an asteroid called B-612, which has been sighted only once—in 1909, when a Turkish astronomer discovered it.

However, when the Turkish astronomer made an elaborate presentation to the International Astronomical Congress about this discovery, no one took him seriously because he was wearing funny-looking Turkish clothes. However, the regime changed in his country, and the new dictator made it a strict rule to wear European clothes. So, when the astronomer made another presentation in 1920, he was dressed impressively, and everyone believed him.

I have given you these details about the asteroid because of the grown-ups. If you tell them you have made a new friend, they will not ask you how his voice sounds, or what games he likes the best, or if he likes butterflies. For them, what is important is how old he is, how many brothers he has, how much his father earns. These numbers are what makes the grown-ups know about your friend.

More than the beauty and essence of things, grown-ups like facts and figures and labels.

Grown-ups need more proof than the fact that a prince asked for a sheep. However, if you told them that the prince came from Asteroid B-612, they would believe you.

I could have written this story like a fairy tale and begun: 'Once upon a time, there was a prince who lived on a planet not much bigger than a house. He was in need of a sheep...'

But I want my book to be taken seriously. It has been six years since he left with the sheep. I describe him here so that I do not forget him. I am afraid that if I forget him, I will be just like the grown-ups—interested only in facts and numbers.

I am afraid my friend thought me to be a lot like him. But I am not. I cannot see the sheep through the box, as I have had to grow up.

Each day, I learnt something new about the little prince's planet; why he left and about his journey. Mostly, it was because of some odd comment he made. This is how I learnt of the baobab trouble.

On the third day after I had met him, the little prince asked, 'Sheeps eat little bushes, no?'

When I said yes, he enquired again, 'Does that mean, they also eat baobabs?'

On the little prince's planet, baobab seedlings have to be uprooted when they are small. The baobab tree is huge and its roots can bore through the planet. If you don't tend to it immediately, you will never get rid of it.

'It is a matter of discipline,' he said. 'It is a boring work, but easy.'

He then told me about a lazy man who neglected three tiny bushes... Here is a picture of what happened to the planet. Even though I don't

like to sound preachy, I would say here, 'Children, watch out for the baobabs.'

The little prince must have been very lonely, since the only entertainment on his planet was watching sunsets. This I came to know on the morning of the fourth day, when he said, 'Come, let us go look at a sunset.'

It was only when I said, 'We will have to wait till the evening for the sunset,' that he remembered that he was not home.

He then told me that sunsets can cheer people up when they are sad. In the same breath, he said he had once seen forty-four sunsets in one day! You see, on his planet, a person can see a sunset just by moving a few steps.

But the little prince refused to tell me if he had been sad on the day that he saw forty-four sunsets.

On the fifth day, I found out the little prince's secret.

It all started with the question, 'Does the sheep eat flowers?'

'A sheep,' I answered, 'eats anything within its reach.'

'Even flowers with thorns?'

'Yes.'

'Then what use are the thorns?'

I didn't have an answer.

'What use are the thorns if they can't protect the flower?' he asked again.

I didn't know. I have to admit, at that moment I was more worried about my engine and that I had so little water left. So I just yelled at him that I had more serious matters than useless thorns to think about.

He just looked at me thunderstruck and said, 'You talk just like the grown-ups.'

This is when I found out that he loved the flower he spoke of. And I realized how important it was for the little prince that I took love more seriously than some ugly engine.

I came to know this flower better over the next few days. Unlike the other flowers on the prince's planet, which had only one ring of petals, this unique flower with thorns emerged from a huge bud with carefully arranged petals.

As the prince told me more about the flower, I considered it very vain and demanding: she wanted the prince to tend to her every morning with fresh water and protect her from cold drafts with a glass globe in the evening. However, one day, the prince caught the flower on the verge of a lie, and began to doubt her love. This made the prince so unhappy and so lonely that he decided to leave his planet to explore the universe.

'I should have never listened to her,' he told me. 'I should have judged her from her deeds and not her words. I was too young to know how to love her.'

On the morning of the day of his departure, he started putting his planet in order. He carefully cleaned out the two active volcanoes—he uses these two to heat his breakfast—and the extinct one as well, just in case, and pulled out all the baobab shoots that he could find. Then, he went to tend to the flower one last time.

'Goodbye,' the prince said to the flower.

At first, she refused to reply, but eventually said, 'I am sorry.'

Then, she told the little prince that she loved him and that she had been silly not to show it. She assured him she would manage without him, and encouraged him to go, even though she did not know when they would meet again.

After leaving home, the little prince visited several neighbouring asteroids.

The first one was inhabited by a king without any subjects.

Happy to finally have a subject, the king ordered the prince not to yawn. But when the prince said he couldn't help yawning, the king change his order.

'I order you to yawn,' he said.

The king then made a sweeping gesture indicating his planet, other planets and all the stars, and told the little prince that he reigned over everything and that everything obeyed him.

The prince was amazed by the king's words, and believed the king. So he asked the king for a favour.

'Would you please order the sun to set?' he said.

Obviously, the king could not do that. He said, 'One must require from each one the duty which each one can perform.'

Thus, the prince realized that the king wasn't all that powerful, and that he tailored his 'orders' to match the world around him.

So, the prince decided to leave, and would not change his mind, even when the king promised to make him the Minister of Justice.

As the prince continued on his journey, he said to himself, 'Grown-ups are strange.'

On the second planet lived a conceited man.

When he saw the prince from afar, he exclaimed, 'I'm about to be visited by an admirer.'

You see, vain people think everyone they meet are their admirers.

'Good morning,' the little prince said to the man and commented on his hat.

'The hat is made for salutes,' the conceited man told the prince. He then told the prince to clap his hands. When the prince did so, the conceited man raised his hat in salute.

'This is more fun than my visit to the king,' the little prince thought and then clapped his hands again.

The man raised his hat in salute again.

But within five minutes, the little prince grew tired of this game.

'Do you really admire me?' the man asked the prince.

But the prince didn't know what admire meant, so he asked the vain man to explain.

'To admire me means you regard me as the handsomest, the best dressed most intelligent person on this planet,' the man said.

When the prince told him he was the only man on the planet, the vain man said, 'Admire me just the same.'

'I admire you,' the prince said indifferently and left.

'Grown-ups are odd,' was his parting thought.

On the third planet, the prince met a man in a stupor, who had one collection of empty bottles, and another of full bottles.

'What are you doing?' the little prince asked the planet's sole inhabitant.

'I'm drinking,' came the reply.

'Why are you drinking?'

'To forget.'

'To forget what?' asked the little prince.

'To forget that I am ashamed,' the drunkard replied.

'Ashamed of?'

'Ashamed of drinking.'

This conversation confused the prince and he walked away, reinforcing his belief that the grown-ups are strange.

The fourth planet was occupied by a businessman, who was too busy to even raise his head to look at the visitor.

The businessman was counting, and he kept counting even while talking to the little prince.

'What are you counting?' the prince asked. He got no answer.

'Five-hundred-and-one million, six-hundred-twenty-two thousand, seven-hundred-thirty-one,' the businessman kept counting.

Finally, after the prince asked twice more, the businessman said, 'those' and pointed in the general direction away from him.

As it turned out, the businessman was counting stars, and claimed that he owned them all!

For the little prince, that didn't make sense.

'But, how can you own these stars?' he asked.

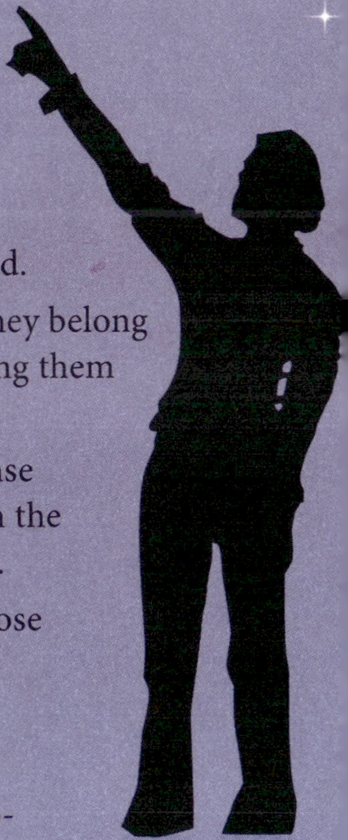

'If not me, to whom do these stars belong?' the man asked, somewhat crankily.

'To nobody,' the prince replied.

'So, it stands to reason that they belong to me because I thought of owning them first,' the man said.

For the prince, that made sense as much as the conversation with the drunkard on the previous planet.

'What will you do with all those stars?' he asked.

'Why, I will write down this number—five-hundred-and-one million, six hundred-twenty-two-

thousand, seven-hundred-thirty-one—on a piece of paper and put it in a bank,' the man replied.

'What use is that? I own a flower, which I water every day. I own three volcanoes, which I clean out every week. So my owning is of some use. Of what use are you to the stars?' asked the prince.

The businessman didn't have an answer.

The prince then walked away, now convinced that the grown-ups were weird.

The fifth planet, smallest of them all, was a bit strange.

There was just enough space for a street lamp and a lamplighter.

For the prince though the lamplighter was not as absurd as the king without any subjects, the vain person, the businessman or even the drunkard he met on previous planets. The prince thought, 'Even if it is strange that there is a street lamp in a place where there are no people, not even a house, at least the lamplighter's job has true meaning. When he lights the lamp, it means he's brought it to life and when he puts it out, it means he has put the lamp to sleep.'

Just then, the lamplighter put out the lamp, and the prince asked him why.

'Those are the orders,' replied the lamplighter, and wished him good morning.

'What orders?'

'That I put out my lamp,' said the lamplighter, and said good evening just as he lit the lamp again.

'So why light it again?'

'Those are the orders,' said the lamplighter.

So the prince was confused and asked the lamplighter to explain.

The lamplighter's job was to put out the lamp in the morning and light it again at night, but over the years, the small planet turned faster and faster—now it turned so fast that one minute it was night and the next minute was day. By the time the lamplighter put out his lamp, it was night again. So, his work was never done.

The prince came up with an idea to help the man rest, 'Your planet is so small that three strides will take you all the way around it. To be always in the sunshine, you need only walk along rather slowly. When you want to rest, you will walk—and the day will last as long as you like.'

However, this plan would not allow the lamplighter to sleep, which was all he wanted to do.

So, the little prince continued on his journey, feeling sad that he was leaving the one person he could have been friends with, had there been enough room on the planet for two people.

But the real reason for the prince's sadness was that he was leaving a planet that had 1,440 sunsets in a day.

The sixth planet was by far the largest one the little prince had visited. There lived an old gentleman who wrote big books.

When the old man saw the little prince coming, he thought he was being visited by an explorer.

'Where do you come from?' asked the old man of the little prince.

In reply, the prince asked what that big book was and what he was doing with it.

'I'm a geographer,' said the man.

Because the little prince didn't know what a 'geographer' was, the old man explained that a geographer is a person who knows the location of all the rivers, towns, seas, mountains and deserts.

But had the old man visited any a river on his planet?

No.

A town?

No.

Any sea?

No.

A mountain, any desert?

No and no.

Why? Because the man believed that being a geographer, he was too important to explore. He never left his desk. According to the old man, explorations were done by explorers. The geographer collects information from explorers and then, if the explorer is of sound character, investigates the explorer's discoveries.

The geographer now wanted the little prince to describe his planet and be an explorer for him.

The prince then started telling the geographer about the three volcanoes—including the extinct one—and the flower on his planet. The geographer, however, refused to record it, calling it 'ephemeral'.

The prince, now completely worried about his flower, which only had four thorns to protect her, decided to leave this planet and asked the geographer for a suggestion.

The geographer suggested the Earth.

So, the prince's seventh planet was the Earth.

Now, the Earth has a actual amount of grown-ups—hundreds of kings, thousands of geographers, hundreds of thousands of businessmen, thousands of thousands of tipplers and even more conceited men.

In fact, before the invention of electricity, a sizeable army of lamplighters were needed for the street lamps.

That would have been the sight—when this army of lamplighters would get to start their business when the sun sets. Starting from New Zealand and Australia and slowly moving to China and Siberia, then to Russia and Indies, then to Africa and Europe, then after that to South America and to North America. This order would never be changed any day.

The single lamplighters of North Pole and South Pole would have to work only twice a year.

Now, although grown-ups on the Earth think they are very important people who occupy a lot of space, the truth is that the entire humanity can be filled in one Pacific islet. But, if you tell the grown-ups that, they will never believe you.

Now, when the little prince arrived on the Earth, he was quite pleased to not find anyone. However, after a while passed, he began to wonder if he had come to the wrong planet.

But right then, he saw a coil of gold flash across the desert.

It was a snake.

The prince asked the snake what planet it was.

'This is the Earth; this is Africa,' the snake replied.

'Are there no people on the Earth?'

The snake replied that it was the desert and there were no people in the desert, and that the Earth is large.

As they continued talking, the prince called the snake a funny-looking animal.

'You're no thicker than a finger!' he said.

'But I am more powerful than the finger of a king,' the snake replied.

The little prince smiled.

'You are not very powerful. You don't even have any feet to travel.'

'I can carry you farther than any ship could take you,' said the snake.

Then, the snake told the prince, 'You are innocent and true; I can help you. Someday, if you grow too homesick for your own planet, I can help.'

Then, as the prince explored the desert, he met a flower with three petals. She had seen a caravan many years before, but thought that she had seen all the men in the world.

'There are about six or seven of them,' she said. 'But one never knows where to find them. The wind blows them away as they have no roots.'

The only mountains the prince had ever known were the three volcanoes, which came up to his knees. And he used the extinct volcano as a footstool.

So when he saw a very high mountain, he decided to climb it, to see the whole planet and all the people at one glance. But all he heard was his own echo. By the end of this adventure, he thought of the Earth as completely dry, pointed, harsh and forbidding, and that all the people were quite dull since they only repeated what you said to them.

He walked for a while and reached a garden filled with roses, just like his rose back at home. He was shocked! His flower had told him that she was the only one of her kind in the universe; and here were five thousand of them, all alike, in one single garden!

He then thought of how his flower would react to see this.

'She would cough and pretend to be dying, to avoid being laughed at. And I would tend to her, or else she really would die,' he said to himself.

He continued thinking, 'I thought that I was rich, and had a unique flower; but all I have are a common rose, and three volcanoes that come up to my knees... That doesn't make me a very great prince...'

And he lay down in the grass and cried. This was when the fox came along.

The prince found the fox very pretty and wanted the fox to play with him. The fox refused saying it wasn't 'tamed'.

The prince then asked the fox to explain what tamed meant. The fox said that tamed meant to have ties, to have relationships and then asked the little prince to 'tame' him.

The prince said, 'I would love to, but I can't as I don't have enough time. I have friends to discover and things to understand.'

'One only understands the things that one tames,' said the fox. 'Men no longer have any time to understand anything. They buy ready-made things at shops. But there are no shops to buy friends, so men don't have friends any more. If you want a friend, tame me.'

Then the fox told the prince how to tame him: the prince had to sit at a little distance from the fox, from where the fox would look at the prince from the corner of his eyes. Every day, the prince should sit a little closer and the prince should be patient with the fox.

'And you will say nothing. Words are the source of misunderstanding,' the fox said.

So the prince came back the next day, and the next day, and eventually tamed the fox.

When it was time for the prince to leave, the fox became sad, but said that—even though it made him sad—he was happy to have been 'tamed'. The fox also told the prince to go look at the rose garden once again.

There, the prince realized the importance of being tamed and told the roses, 'You are beautiful, but you are not my rose. Because I have watered her, put her under glass globe and sheltered her, she is so much more important than all of you. And even if she grumbles or boasts or even keeps quiet, she is my rose.'

And then the prince went back to meet the fox, who gave him some advice as a parting gift.

'It is only with the heart that one can see rightly; what is essential is invisible to the eye,' the fox said.

The fox then said that the prince's flower was special because of all the effort he had put into their relationship, and added, 'You are responsible for what you have tamed.'

Next, the prince met a railway switchman.

'What do you do here?' the prince asked.

The railway switchman explained that he sorted out travellers on trains by sending them right or left.

Just then a train passed by at great speed.

The prince asked, 'They seem to be in a hurry. What are they looking for?'

'No one knows,' said the switchman.

When the prince saw another train pass by in the opposite direction, he asked, 'Are they coming back already? Were they not happy where they were?'

'No one is happy with where they are,' replied the switchman.

'No one even bothers to look out the window anymore. They are busy sleeping or yawning,' the switchman continued. 'Only the children look out the window now.'

'Only the children know what they are looking for,' said the prince.

The switchman agreed and called them lucky.

Then, the prince met a merchant who sold a pill that could quench thirst. According to the merchant, one only needed to take one pill a week, so the pill saved fifty-three minutes every week.

'And what would I do with those fifty-three minutes?' asked the prince.

'Anything you like,' came the reply.

'If I had those fifty-three minutes, I would walk up to a spring of fresh water,' said the prince.

It was now the eighth day since my accident in the desert. I was listening to the merchant's story as I was drinking the last drop of my water.

At last, I said to the prince, 'These memories of your journey are very charming, but I am yet to finish repairs on my plane and I have no more water to drink. In this condition, I too shall be very happy to walk up to a spring of fresh water.'

The prince—who never seemed to be hungry or thirsty—then suggested that we should both look for a well.

So, that is what we set out to do.

Hours went by, and soon it was night; but we still hadn't found a well. The prince and I were both very tired, and finally, we sat down on the sand.

There, we talked about the beauty of the stars, the desert—the beauty of the invisible. The stars were beautiful because of an unseen flower and the desert was beautiful because of a hidden well within it.

The prince soon fell asleep. That is when I understood how fragile the little prince was, and how loyal he was to the little flower. I wanted to protect him from any harm; he looked like even a strong wind could harm him.

Thus, I carried the little prince in my arms and began to walk. At daybreak, I found a well.

Strangely, the well looked like one we would find in a village: there was a bucket tied to a rope which went over the pulley—all ready for use.

The prince lowered the bucket into the well, and said that we had awakened the well, and that it was now singing. I didn't want the little prince to tire himself out, so I took over the task of drawing water. The prince was thirsty so he drank the water that I had pulled out. After that, I drank the water too.

All this while the prince was quiet. But after I finished drinking, the prince asked me to draw a muzzle for his sheep and then set out to criticize my drawings of the baobabs and the fox.

Then he told me that the next day would be the anniversary since his arrival on the Earth and that he had landed not far from the place where we were.

That made me sad, even though I did not know why.

Then, realization struck!

'You were on your way back to your landing spot when you met me a week ago, weren't you?' I asked him.

He didn't answer, but flushed. And I was frightened. Just then, he told me to return to my engine and come back the next evening.

There is an old wall next to the well. When I came back from working on the engine the next evening, I saw the prince sitting on it and talking to someone—even though I couldn't see who it was.

When I neared the wall, I heard the prince say, 'You will see my tracks beginning in the sand and you will wait for me there. I shall be there tonight.'

Then, he said, 'You have good poison? You won't make me suffer for long?'

And that is when I saw a yellow snake—the kind that can kill you within half a minute—at the foot of the wall. But as I was reaching for my gun to shoot the thing, it carelessly slipped into the sand.

The prince saw me and told me that he was returning home today, just like I would be, very soon.

I asked him, how he knew that I had successfully finished repairing my engine.

He didn't answer me, but told me that he was returning home, which was much farther away, and much harder to reach.

And I couldn't bear to let him go. I told him that I wanted to hear him laugh again.

He said to me, 'Tonight, it will be a year since I landed on the Earth. My star will be right above the place where I landed.'

But I still didn't want to let him go.

The little prince then gave me a gift.

'At night when you look at the stars, my star will be among them; and because you don't know which one is my star, all of them will be your friends. And, in one of them, I will be laughing. So, for you, because you wouldn't know which one, all the stars will be laughing.'

'And when you are sad,' he continued, 'you will be content that you knew me. You will always be my friend. You will, sometimes, want to laugh, with me. So you will look out the window just for that and laugh looking at the stars. People will be surprised and you could always tell them that stars make you happy.'

The little prince then went silent.

After a while, he told me, 'You know, tonight? Don't come.'

I told him I couldn't leave him alone.

He told me that it might look like he was suffering, and dying.

'Do not come to see that,' he said.

I told him I couldn't leave him alone.

He told me he was worried that the snake could bite me, but I didn't want to leave him.

That night, he set out without making a sound. When I caught up with him, he was walking very quickly and firmly.

He saw me and said, 'There you are. It was wrong of you to come. You will suffer. It might look like I am dead.'

I said nothing.

'This body, it is too heavy. I can't carry it that far,' he told me.

I kept mum.

'It will look like an old abandoned shell,' he said.

Again, I said nothing.

Finally, he sat down and told me, 'My flower—I am responsible for her. She is so weak. She has four thorns but no protection against the world.'

Then he got up and took one step.

There was a flash of yellow near his ankle. Then gently, he fell. There was no noise because of the sand.

It has been six years since that night. I have never told anyone this story. All I told anybody who met me after that accident was that I was tired.

However, I take a bit of comfort in knowing that the little prince did make it back to his planet: when I went looking for him at daybreak, I didn't find his body. It was not such a heavy body after all.

Now, it is true that I love to listen to the stars. But I also wonder about the sheep. You see, I forgot to draw a strap for the muzzle.

But that is neither here nor there.

All I have to say is that in case you happen to travel to Africa and to the Sahara, wait for a moment under the stars. If you see a little man with golden hair who laughs and asks questions, you will know who he is.

Other Titles in the Series

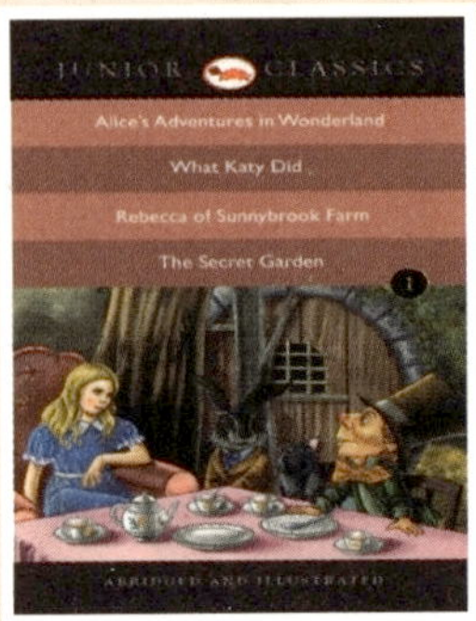

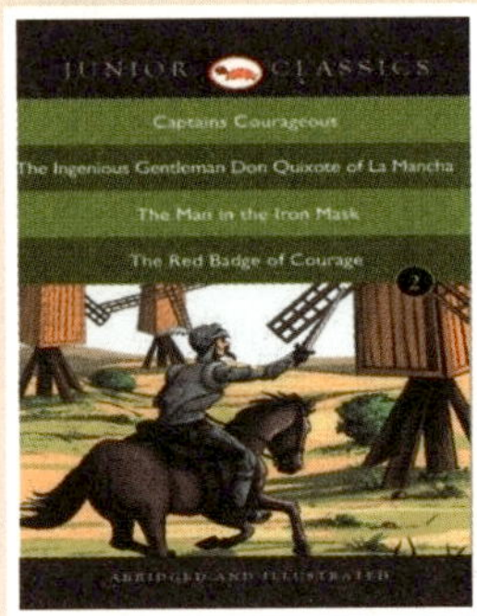

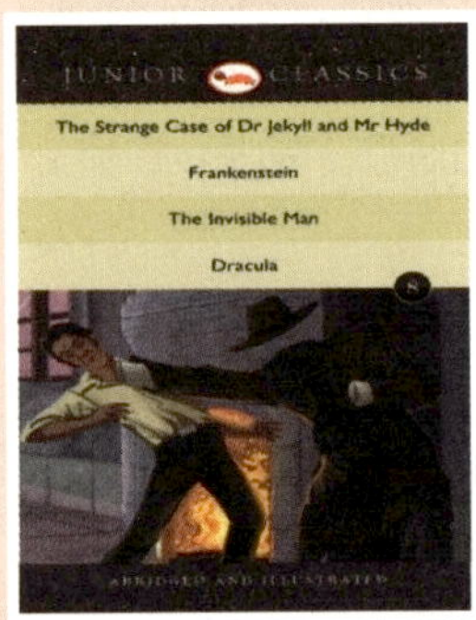